W9-DEV-993

The Mercy Room

A Novel

Gilles Rozier

Translated from the French by Anthea Bell

Little, Brown and Company
New York   Boston

The
Mercy Room

Copyright © 2003 by Éditions Denoël
Translation copyright © 2005 by Anthea Bell

All rights reserved. No part of this book may be reproduced in any form
or by any electronic or mechanical means, including information storage
and retrieval systems, without permission in writing from the publisher,
except by a reviewer who may quote brief passages in a review.

Little, Brown and Company
Time Warner Book Group
1271 Avenue of the Americas, New York, NY 10020
Visit our Web site at www.twbookmark.com

The characters and events in this book are fictitious. Any similarity to real
persons, living or dead, is coincidental and not intended by the author.

First U.S. Edition: March 2006

Un amour sans résistance was first published in
France in 2003 by Éditions Denoël
First published in Great Britain as *Love Without Resistance*
in 2005 by Little, Brown and Company

Library of Congress Cataloging-in-Publication Data

Rozier, Gilles.
 [Amour sans résistance. English]
 The mercy room : a novel / Gilles Rozier ;
translated from the French by Anthea Bell. — 1st ed.
 p. cm.
 ISBN-10: 0-316-15973-5 (hardcover)
 ISBN-13: 978-0-316-15973-9 (hardcover)
 I. Bell, Anthea. II. Title.

PQ2718.O95A813 2006
843'.92 — dc22   2005020370

10 9 8 7 6 5 4 3 2 1

Q-MB

Book designed by Brooke Koven

Printed in the United States of America

For Jean

Ein Fichtenbaum steht einsam
Im Norden, auf kahler Höh.
Ihn schläfert; mit weisser Decke
Umhüllen ihn Eis und Schnee.

Er träumt von einer Palme
Die, fern im Morgenland,
Einsam und schweigend trauert
Auf brennender Felsenwand.

A fir stands tall and lonely
On barren northern heights.
It slumbers in white covers
Of freezing snow and ice.

The fir dreams of a palm tree
In distant eastern lands,
Silent, alone, in mourning
On burning rocks it stands.

— Heinrich Heine

The Mercy Room

1

IF YOU WANT ME to tell you the story, put some Schumann on; the music will bring my memories back. *Lieder*, yes . . . let's start with *Schöne Wiege meiner Leiden*. TUMty TUMty TUMty TUMty — four of the most inspired of all German trochees. I'll dim the light. Let the tea steep for a few minutes, would you? I like a drop of milk in it, Chinese tea. This is my grandmother's teapot. Very old, although it may not look it. It was a wedding present from her godmother, just back from Hong Kong, where her husband had been working for an English firm. My grandmother married a year before my mother's birth, in 1889, so you can see how old it is . . .

XOXOX

The fat one in the middle is my mother. On her left is my sister Isabelle with her husband, Jean-Louis, next to her. On Isabelle's lap, her daughter France. She can't have been more than a year old at the time. On my mother's right, my other sister, Anne; her husband had already been liquidated by the Resistance. The tallest boy there is François, Isabelle's eldest, with her second son, Marcel, beside him. And little Alfred. And that's me. The photo was taken outside my mother's house. Well, the house was all of ours, but mostly hers. There was a porch with steps up to it; my mother had it demolished after the war, but you can still see the windows and the acacia tree. My father was a prisoner in Germany.

The photographer was Volker Hammerschimmel, an SS man. He was fucking my sister Anne, if you'll forgive the expression. I can't think how else to put it. She used to cry out loud with pleasure up on the second floor. The crystal chandelier in the drawing room jingled in time to the thrusts of the Boche's loins. The war was so dismal a period, you had to enjoy yourself somehow. My sister was in mourning, poor thing. She screwed to take her mind off it. She loved being penetrated by the enemy, and proclaimed it out loud. She was like her country: free for the taking.

When the Liberation came, a neighbor raped my sister Anne, cheered on by everyone in our part of town. It hap-

pened outside our garden gate. I had joined the crowd.
Anne was unrecognizable, her head shaved bare. She looked
scrawny; she was stark naked. It was the first time I'd ever
seen her naked, not just the skin of her skull but her whole
body, all of her. The neighbor was lying on top of her in
the middle of the road. All you saw of the rapist was his
buttocks, two rounded watermelons, he was regional cross-
country ski champion. My sister had never undressed in
front of me — we weren't the kind of family where you
showed yourself — yet she had been stripped naked in my
head every time she gave herself to Volker. She used to utter
such loud cries, she might as well have flung the second-floor
window open wide to show her breasts, her belly, her sex.

My sister said she was traumatized by this postwar rape.
Human beings react strangely. It didn't strike her as shocking to make love with the Führer's representative on earth
daily, sometimes twice a day — never at night because he
slept at the barracks — but three or four little thrusts of the
neighbor's prick one morning before aperitif time broke
something inside her. It was the other way around with me:
I watched the cross-country skier poking at my naked sister
on the road and the scene seemed less violent than the loud
cries that had punctuated our war. And yet in a way, Anne
and her SS officer had been useful to me by giving the family home a certain immunity. So to some extent I was an
accessory to the crime of which Anne stood accused, and
which she paid for with that public rape. When the Liberation came, it wasn't easy to explain all the comings and

goings that had gone on during the Occupation in our house with its red shutters, all that climbing up the stairs and down to the cellar.

My mother spent a lot of time in the kitchen next to the living room, on the first floor. There wasn't much for her to cook in her saucepans, but she carried on with her old habits, just as someone with an amputated hand still mentally sweeps a crumb off the table with his forefinger. My mother stayed in the kitchen, cleaning most of the time. When my sister started moaning, I would see the expression on my mother's face change, and the rhythm of her pan scourer became more frenzied in time to the jolting of the crystal chandelier in the drawing room. My mother was no longer the strong, authoritarian head of the family, but a slave bending her back beneath her tormentor's blows. Every one of my sister's cries was like a cudgel coming down.

I used to leave the house when Volker arrived. I didn't want to suffer the affront of knowing that the enemy was pouring his seed into my sister's body. But strange as it may seem, Volker often slipped in very discreetly, and I sometimes realized he was there only when the chandelier began to shake. Given the time it took to put on my coat, tie my shoelaces and comb my hair quickly in front of the hall mirror, I would be obliged to hear my sister's first moans before I was through the garden gate. As I left the house, going down the porch steps, I would look up at the kitchen window and see my mother, her expression fixed, frantically scouring the already spotless frying pan.

For my mother never said anything. She could have slapped my sister, called her a tart, a slut, a soldier's whore, a prostitute in the pay of the Boche and God knows what else, but such insults stuck in her throat. My mother was incapable of chastising her precious youngest child. She was usually quick to raise her hand in anger and had disciplined her other children severely. Had she sworn never to touch my sister Anne except to caress her? She had always indulged her, and Anne took full advantage of it. From childhood she had done exactly as she liked without ever being reprimanded. She trampled the flowers in the garden and ate the raspberries before they were picked, leaving none for anyone else. She often stole bicycles in the neighborhood.

At fourteen she ran away for the first time, following a construction worker's son who was off to harvest grapes in the south. When she came home, I could tell from my mother's face that Anne was no longer a virgin. For several weeks, my mother seemed nervous, as if worrying about something, and then one day she was suddenly all smiles again. I asked Anne if she knew why our mother was so relieved, and she told me: She isn't going to be a grandma just yet.

Anne didn't go back to school after this escapade, but she was spared having to work. She spent her evenings dancing, her mornings sleeping, and her afternoons flirting. She was free to do anything she liked, and she knew no bounds. Yet our parents had been strict with Isabelle and me. We were kept under permanent supervision.

My elder sister had met a boy from the southwest, some godforsaken dump in Gascony; you couldn't get there by either train or car in under sixteen hours. She married him in haste to get out of the parental line of fire. On the day when that photo was taken she was visiting, which was unusual. It was Easter time, I think, but she left that same evening. We hardly ever saw her, and spent the war without her. When the national territory was cut in two, she didn't mind: a bold demarcation line traced across the map of France separated her from us, a border like a cordon sanitaire. Myself, I stayed within range of my mother. I was rather a docile character. My father was away for the whole of the war, first at the front, then as a prisoner in Germany, near Idar-Oberstein.

Would our war have been different if my father hadn't been a prisoner? You can't remake history, you have to take the world as it is with all the dead on its battlefields, the emigrations, famines, purges, and exterminations. My father wasn't entirely with us even before the war. He went to work, he came home, he did some gardening on Sundays and summer evenings. In winter he bottled his wine in the cellar; he went to Mass on Sundays and took Communion, a reflex left over from his childhood. When he got up in the morning he said, "How are you?" and didn't wait to hear the answer. He lived in a world of his own, what world you couldn't really be sure, double-locked behind an invisible door: it was a tenuous veil but enough to make him inaccessible. When I sometimes asked, as a child, "What are you thinking about, Papa?" he would say, "I was just falling asleep," or "The roses are very red this year."

Early in the evening on Christmas and New Year's Day, after sitting at the table all afternoon and pretending to join in the conversation, he would suddenly get up and say he was going to make onion soup, another reflex, almost an instinct, like taking Communion but no doubt performed with more sincerity, because he flung himself into it whole-heartedly, browning onions, adding water and white wine, toasting bread, grating cheese — Comté rather than Gruyère, because it tastes better and it's French — putting it all in the oven and, most important, most important of all, stirring it seven times while it was still in the oven before adding the toast to the whole dish. His onion soup was delicious, but is the flavor of a certain dish enough to remember a father by?

My mother was always there. In my childhood, during the war, after the war, too, although nothing was the same then. She was a rock, a fixture in her home, as if the house had been built around her.

When the Legion of French Volunteers was founded to oppose Bolshevism, Anne's husband was among the first in the region to join. He wasn't fit to be called up in 1939 — his health was too poor — but he wanted to serve France. The

Legion accepted asthmatics. As the wife of a volunteer, Anne put on airs for several months. She acted as if it was a *sous-préfet* she'd married and bought herself a new hat. Anne and her husband made new friends among supporters of the Vichy government. The Maréchal had delegated full powers in our part of town to my sister, and she terrorized the neighborhood through the agency of her husband. If a neighbor or tradesman failed to obey her, she would give him a black look; reprisals were not long in coming to the dissident.

One morning my sister and my brother-in-law were breakfasting on the porch. It was a beautiful day, the acacia was covered with flowers. A car drew up outside the garden gate. A man with his face exposed produced a gun. *Tac-a-tac-a-tac-a-tac.* He fired at the couple. He hit the husband right in the head and missed my sister, but it was too late to try again. The car peeled off, and Anne was left sitting there as if turned to stone, splashed with her husband's blood. My brother-in-law never had time to go and die of cold on the steppes of Russia or to join the Milice paramilitaries, as he certainly would have done had he lived.

The head of I forget what local faction delivered an address at the funeral. He swore to bring the guilty men to justice. His words about the anti-France movement thundered through the cathedral. Anne wore black, a dress with long sleeves down to her wrists and a high collar. It was summer and the heat was scorching. The next week Anne had altered the dress to suit the season: short sleeves, plunging neckline. A few snips of the scissors, a lift of the hem, and four gilt buttons sufficed to smarten up her mourning garb. She began going out a great deal. Her status as the widow of a collaborator exempted her from the curfew. She went to cabarets where fashionable singers contributed to the war effort by entertaining the men of our conqueror's army. She came home in the wee hours, often drunk. She would talk in a loud voice as she got out of the car that brought her back, sometimes speaking a few words in broken German, a language she had never been able to learn properly. A few weeks later Volker entered her like a knife going through butter.

2

I TAUGHT GERMAN, a noble profession. A beautiful language, perfect for honing the ability of good students. I loved its literature. I had read everything: Lessing, Goethe, Schiller and Kleist, Kant, Nietzsche, Hölderlin, the brothers Grimm, Schelling, Brentano, von Arnim, von Chamisso, Hoffmann, Heine, Büchner, Lou Andreas-Salomé, Schnitzler, Hoffmannsthal, Rilke, Werfel, Wedekind, Lasker-Schüler, Trakl, Döblin, Kafka, Remarque, von Horvath, Jünger, Musil, Hesse, Wassermann, Zweig, Kästner, Benn, Brecht, and I don't know how many more. My library was one of the best in town. Thomas Mann held pride of place there. *Tristan, Tonio Kröger, Buddenbrooks, Königliche Hoheit, Joseph und seine Brüder, Der Zauberberg, Mario und der Zauberer* and above all *Der Tod in Venedig. Death in Venice.*

In Heidelberg in 1930, before Mann was banned by the Nazis, I had bought a fine edition published by S. Fischer of Berlin, and bound in full leather. I perfected my knowledge of German during a year studying literature at Heidelberg University. Mine had been a solitary childhood, and I made no close friendships. Nor had I sought anyone's company in Germany; I preferred to go for walks and sit on a park bench reading. Among the dozens of young people in the Faculty of Literature, however, I had noticed a good-looking, sensitive boy called Hans-Joachim Friedberg.

Most of the students sitting in the university lecture rooms were there because it was what their parents wanted. They let themselves be guided into a course for which they felt no real enthusiasm. They were content to take notes on what the lecturers taught them. As for the rest of it, they were being educated with the opposite sex for the first time in their lives and were feeling their first amorous stirrings. The boys spent their time teasing the girls, the girls were happy to be teased.

Hans-Joachim was different. He didn't distinguish between boys and girls, only between those who were or were not sensitive to art and beauty. Since we thought alike in that way, we soon became friendly. Hans-Joachim's father would have liked him to be a mathematician, but he had gotten his own way and registered in the Faculty of Literature because the German language, the way it was used by writers, and the worlds they offered up were so seductive that they demanded a lifetime of study. Hans-Joachim wanted to be a writer, or a theater director, or perhaps a professor of German literature. He dreamed of filling lecture halls: students would come to hear him the way some people crowd into sports stadiums for a collective, mystical experience.

Hans-Joachim passed on to me a passion for Thomas Mann. I had read almost all of Mann before I met my friend, but he had me rereading *The Magic Mountain* and the others, or rather listening to them, for he would declaim whole pages to me in his room in the evening. I would lie on the bed, which was just like mine. (All the rooms were furnished in the same way, although he and I didn't live in the same building, and no personal touches were allowed; Greater Germany would not have tolerated anything fanciful.) Hans-Joachim would stand there, the open book held at arm's length, and begin to read. The music, the music of Thomas Mann, was like a Schubert quartet. I couldn't decide between closing my eyes, so as to enjoy the text better, and keeping them wide open, for Hans-Joachim was handsome, and I liked to see his face grow animated as he read. He had steely blue eyes with a slightly darker ring around the pupil, and when he spoke on those evenings, his eyes sometimes left the book in his hands and turned on me, lively, expressive eyes. His skin was smooth and delicate, like the skin of a perfectly ripe peach which

you know will come off the tree easily if you hold it in your
fingertips.

The reading lasted hours. My friend was possessed of myste-
rious energy; he seldom paused for breath, and the text flowed
exactly as Mann had conceived it, limpid, crystalline. Hans-
Joachim could easily have been an actor. After several chap-
ters he would stop short. He would remain on his feet for a
few moments while the sound of the words died away, and
then lie down on the bed beside me. Stretched full length on
the mattress, his neck slightly turned so that his head could
rest against the partition, he would examine the pattern of
the paper on the wall facing us. His breath came fast. He
was making up for all the oxygen he hadn't stopped to take
in as he read. Slowly, his breathing would calm down, and
Hans-Joachim would fall asleep.

When I knew he couldn't catch me doing it, I would turn
my head to watch him sleeping. I stole a little of his slumber,
but only with my eyes. I gazed at the sweep of his brown
lashes, the flesh of his mouth, its carmine contrasting with
his warm-hued rosy skin. I could have stayed there all night
watching him, but I felt guilty for spying on him like that. I
would stop after twenty minutes or so, keeping my unas-
suaged longings to myself, and return discreetly to my own
room, slipping along the corridors and up and down stairs
quick as a snake, so as not to incur the dorm prefect's wrath,
my copy of *Death in Venice* in my hand.

Back in my own room, I put it under my pillow. I wouldn't have opened it then for anything in the world, preferring to leave my German friend the pleasure of reading it to me. I washed, and the washcloth I passed over my body was like an instrument of purification after those moments of guilty joy, but I was sorry that it removed the last trace of that delicious ambiance from my skin. To me, the meaning of *Death in Venice* was those moments of furtive happiness in Heidelberg. Later, down in the burrow I made myself in occupied France, I reread Thomas Mann; I could hear Hans-Joachim's voice as my eye ran over the printed lines. I can no longer see his gestures, they have faded; I can hardly even remember his scent.

We did not correspond much after my year in Germany. Perhaps we wanted to keep the luster of those months of our lives undimmed. After war was declared I didn't try to find out what had become of Hans-Joachim. He was German, I loved my country, we were at war. He was the enemy.

Hans-Joachim was with me when I bought that copy of *Death in Venice*. The bookseller, an elderly man who seemed to know by heart every line of the books he sold, had wrapped it in tissue paper, and I left it still wrapped until night fell. I had dined with my friend in the dorm cafeteria. Then we went to my room, evading the prefect's vigilance, and Hans-Joachim snatched up the book as if it were something we had both secretly been desiring since morning. He liberated the work from its veil of tissue paper, which fell, silently wafting through the air. Hans-Joachim opened the book at the first page and began to read aloud.

Der Tod in Venedig, Novelle von Thomas Mann. Erstes Kapitel. Gustav Aschenbach, oder von Aschenbach, wie seit seinem fünfzigsten Geburtstag amtlich sein Name lautete, hatte an einem Frühlingsnachmittag des Jahres 19.., das unserem Kontinent monatelang eine so gefahrdrohende Miene zeigte, von seiner Wohnung in der Prinzregentenstrasse zu München aus, allein einen weiteren Spaziergang unternommen. *

Death in Venice became my bedtime reading. When the Germans occupied the southern zone of France I did not actually keep it on my bedside table; they would not have approved. It wasn't the only title to leave my bedroom. I took banned authors down to the cellar. Heine, von Horvath, Arnold and Stefan Zweig, Wassermann, Werfel, Schnitzler, Thomas and Heinrich Mann, the enemies of the eternal German Reich. In what way they were its enemies I didn't understand, I supposed for being Jewish, or Jewish-influenced; I didn't really grasp the significance of those terms very well. In general I hated not understanding something, but this was an era of verbal confusion and slick slogans. I didn't try

---

* For this and all further translations please see pages 151–153.

to pin down the fallacious argument behind the ban, but bowed to it and made my own arrangements.

I fixed up a reading room for myself at the back of our wine cellar. Using some planks that were lying about in the laundry room, an old armchair exiled to the attic because its leather upholstery was so badly worn, and a little office reading lamp, I created a private place for myself and my Nazi rejects. The lamp cast a very concentrated pool of light. I could go down to the cellar by night to read and switch it on, and it would light up my book, but for all but a few feet around me the place remained plunged in darkness. I reached my hiding place through a little arched opening in the wall in the darkest part of the wine cellar, and I had to go down on all fours like an animal to get through it. I had hidden this entrance with some empty crates which I could easily put back in front of the opening once I was inside. For extra security I also blocked it up with some paving stones that I had discreetly gathered, day by day, from a road-building site on my way home from school. Who could possibly find the place where my banned writers lay in hiding? Who would ever think of searching the home of a collaborator who was an SS man's mistress?

I didn't go down to the cellar very often. On Sunday mornings sometimes, while the family was at Mass (I didn't go to church anymore, it was too much of an effort to sit through the vicious sermons delivered by our parish priest, a man who had missed his vocation), or late at night when I couldn't sleep. It took me at least twenty minutes to make myself snug in my library: I had to unblock the opening, slip through, rebuild the barrier of crates and paving stones. So I went down when I could stay there for some time.

Who knew about the existence of this secret place at the back of the cellar? I don't think my sister ever took any interest in the basement of the house, my father was a prisoner of war, the electrician who had repaired the wiring, a cousin on my mother's side, had died at the front in 1940, at Dunkirk. What about my mother? She wouldn't talk, that wasn't like her. She put up with my sister's disgraceful love affair and protected my secret library. I don't know if she even knew about it, but my mother had taught me to tell no tales. There was a phrase she used when we talked too much about other people's business: Keep your own doorstep clean!

As for the books that were left on the shelves in my study, I opened them only to prepare lessons. The idea of this officially approved literature had left me without any wish to read Schiller, Goethe, and all the others who had received the imprimatur of Berlin and Vichy. Although I had not joined the struggle against the occupying forces, I was only interested in those considered to be failures by National Socialist standards. Don't ask me why. Perhaps I had a taste for the forbidden. It had been my habit since childhood to keep everything hidden: my passions, my fears, my disappointments. My mother had set me an example. In our family we didn't wear our hearts on our sleeves. So this blacklist of writers was like a little wind-fall, an excuse for me to make myself a private place where I could read in hiding, which is to say, at liberty, you see?

I had arranged my refugees on the shelves there, with Heine, whose statue in Frankfurt had been knocked down, in pride of place. Most of the volumes were bound in leather, a little quirk of mine: I liked beautiful books. I had taken them to a small workshop in a rather dark street in the old town, all except *Death in Venice*, which I had bought already bound in red leather. I don't know who owned it before me. The title page still bore the traces of a bookplate that the bookseller must have removed before putting the copy on sale again. Whose hands had held it? The dark marks left on the paper by the glue were not enough of a clue for me to reconstruct the childhood of my book. Who had fit it in between the other volumes in his study? A bibliophile who suddenly had to dispose of his collection? An elderly scholar who went on amassing a monumental library even into great old age, and whose children had not scrupled to get rid of his treasures the moment he died? The heir of an aristocrat whose castle had been ransacked by burglars? I liked the idea of having saved *Death in Venice* from its almost certain fate: ending up in flames on one of the pyres built by the Germans in public squares.

On the way to my reading room it was very tempting to pick up a bottle of Romanée-Conti 1932 in passing and to enjoy its contents while I perused a book. I seldom did so, for reasons of prudence, not wanting to arouse any suspicions of my nocturnal activities in the household. I liked resisting the temptation to desecrate a ritual, and left the privileges of the wine cellar and the job of opening the bottles in it to my father. But he was a prisoner in Germany, so I did sometimes uncork a bottle to be with him in spirit, I at the back of a cellar invaded by German books, he working for some illiterate peasant in the Palatine countryside. My father's absence had been a major factor in our war. Who knows how the family's affairs would have gone if he had remained with us? Would my sister have been able to open her legs to the Nazis? And would I have been through the experience I'm about to describe to you at the back of that cellar?

But I'm rambling. When my father came home six years after leaving us, his army kit on his back, he could hardly believe his eyes. His native town was gutted, and his family was in a poor way. I had never been close to my little sister, Anne, but the war was to take us light-years apart, she on the side of the conquered and I more or less on the side of the victims.

In the cellar, the impossibility of taking the chill off the wine, which meant it had to be drunk at a temperature of twelve or thirteen degrees Celsius, helped me to resist the temptation of consuming it in my father's absence. This underground chill also prevented me from staying there to read for very long, because after a certain time my fingers turned numb and I felt the damp seeping into my bones. In winter the temperature of the house itself was not much warmer; we burned prunings from the garden trees, but a lot of them were confiscated as fuel for gasogene-powered vehicles, and we took refuge under the blankets, feet pressed to a hot-water bottle, sheet pulled up to the chin.

Down in the cellar I grappled with two opposing forces: the relaxation of my muscles that came from reading books and the tension caused by the cold and damp. On some nights my mind managed to rise above the problem of the temperature, and I went on reading into the small hours. On others the cold took hold of me before fiction or poetry could carry me away, and I had to abandon my hiding place after barely an hour, chilled to the quick. Then it was impossible to get warm again under the sheets. The damp had gone to the marrow of my bones, and I resigned myself to waiting for morning while trying not to let my teeth chatter for fear of waking Jude, who was a noisy sleeper.

For I had entered into lawful wedlock, as they call it. Lawful it may have been, but as I saw it, wedlock was rather a pathetic business. Jude and I had married as young people did in our day, hardly knowing what we were doing. I was back from Germany and teaching part-time at the local girls' grammar school, simply to earn enough to pay my mother for my keep; only Anne had a claim to free board and lodging. My mother had also found me some private lessons: I was reviewing strong verbs and declensions with Jude, who was taking a course of business studies at a vaguely

Catholic private school, Saint-Pierre, I think, or was it Notre-Dame-du-Bon-Secours? My shy pupil smiled at me during our lessons, replied dutifully to my questions, and looked down when the lady employing me, that is to say Jude's mother, came into the sitting room bringing us a tea tray. I didn't feel any great interest in Jude. We were around the same age, we could have walked together on Sundays, we could have gone to the movies, but I liked my solitude and didn't need anyone else to fill my weekends. I was glad of the bills Jude's mother handed me once a month; when I left with my tutorial fees in my pocket I would cross the road and go into the best bookshop in town. There, I changed money into literature. It was magic.

Toward the end of the year, my mother told me, beaming, how satisfied her friend was with my services. By this I understood only the obvious meaning of the words: I was teaching German to a student who was making good progress. My mother asked questions. What were Jude's likes and dislikes, what color were Jude's eyes? I proved unable to reply. I could have told my mother that Jude knew the list of strong verbs by heart. I had noticed that, like most of our countrymen, my pupil had difficulty in pronouncing the notorious *ch* sound, making it too like *sh,* which always annoyed me. For I had no difficulty with it at all: the delicate hiss, a sound like no other, brought to perfection in the pronoun *Ich,* was all a part of the magic of the German language.

I tried to correct my pupil's pronunciation. "Close your eyes, straighten your shoulders, concentrate and say *Ich.*"

24

The result was a feeble *Ish*. I gave up. I didn't try to make Jude say *Eichhörnchen* — the squirrels could wait to be properly named — nor did I try to find out what kind of person my student was. My interest was in the books that private lessons allowed me to buy and devour. It seems to me now that Jude was indeed courting me, in an unobtrusive way, but at the time I noticed nothing. I didn't want to notice anything.

My mother invited Jude's mother to tea. Jude came, too. My mother hinted that it would be nice if I could look my best, smile, seem just a little bit romantic. I complied. After tea, my mother announced that she liked my young friend. It took me some time to realize that Jude was in the process of joining my family, was going to occupy a place which ought to have aroused either my interest or my distrust: a place beside me in the family tree.

I had never thought of marrying. I had nothing against it, so long as marriage didn't prevent me from reading books and allowed me to keep a certain distance, since I had no intention of giving up my personal independence or my enthusiasms in exchange for conjugal life. I don't remember discussing this subject with Jude before our wedding. We were married one Saturday in summer, nothing very original about it. The town hall, the cathedral, the bishop in his lace nightie, the bridegroom in tails, the bride in white with a long train, gift-wrapped for the occasion, the wedding banquet, some waltzing, the wedding cake. Choosing Zürich as our honeymoon destination was my only contribution to the ceremony; I knew that Thomas Mann was living in exile there and hoped to meet him by chance on a café terrace.

We had been married for several months when my parents-in-law took me aside one day after Sunday lunch. I feared I might be in for a long conversation, and I was in a hurry to get back to the book I was reading. I soon realized that for the last few weeks I had been the subject of many family councils, which Jude's parents now took it upon themselves to report to me. My in-laws talked to me about the wedding night and our relations. I asked, what relations? I had agreed to marry their child, I had never promised any sexual intercourse. This part of my story may sound incredible to you, but I am trying to reconstruct the facts as precisely as I can. I couldn't see why my in-laws suddenly expected me to act indecently when all the premarital transactions had been conducted with the utmost modesty, by dint of euphemism and innuendo, as we sat drinking tea from fine china cups. I remember that we had eaten a great many walnut tarts.

Suddenly I found myself being blamed, if only indirectly, for not giving way to vulgarity, or lending myself to scenes such as those you could see on the racy postcards that the girls at school passed each other under cover of their coats. The woman would be half lying on a damask sofa, her skirts pushed up, presenting her vulva, with its faint suggestion of downy hair, for the delectation of a man standing in front of her, his trousers twisted around his ankles, his buttocks toward the photographer's camera, and his virile member no doubt pointing at his languid prey, but the spectator could only guess at that, because you weren't allowed to show an erect penis at the time.

I had declined to indulge in the games played by these characters, copulating crudely after a dinner washed down with plenty of wine. I respected Jude's character and respectable upbringing too much to do anything so offensive, so likely to taint our relationship. I had listened to the admonishments of the priests I encountered throughout my childhood: the sin of the flesh, dear children, the sin of the flesh! But I now realized that the world expected something else of me, and I felt unable to supply it: sex, the act of copulation, and above that, the production of children. I just couldn't do what I was expected to do. I don't think I had ever felt any desire except for books and the German language.

I preferred Jude fully dressed. I was not interested in my spouse's nudity. Jude could adopt any kind of hairstyle, wear peacock or ostrich feathers, pay particular attention to manicure — I hardly noticed. I could have loved a mind that took pleasure in reading, but as Jude didn't read books, we had little to talk about. Jude was simply there. We bore the same last name, but we had almost nothing in common. Jude's studies had been completed, with an execrable mark in the German exam but good enough grades in other subjects to earn a diploma. The next step was a job in the accounts department of a lumber company.

We lived with my parents, on the second floor of the house, where we had a large bedroom with my study next to it and a bathroom, accommodation for which we paid rent. It would never have occurred to me to move; I had my library here. Jude got on well with my mother and father, and better than I did with my sister Anne. We lived together very comfortably, with never a voice raised between us. I devoted a proper amount of time to my nearest and dearest, dinner with the family every evening, Sundays with my in-laws. I left the company as soon as coffee had been drunk, always very politely, to avoid giving offense, but so firmly that no one would dare to remonstrate with me. And no one did.

I was considered the intellectual of the family, and I fitted the part perfectly. So who could complain? My parents had encouraged me to study, although they had not insisted with my sisters, who were incapable of learning. They had made good use of my diplomas in negotiations with my in-laws, shopkeepers who hoped to rise in the world, and as we were helping them to compensate for the mediocrity of Jude's own educational career, they could hardly complain of deception. Since they could boast of my place in the staff room of the local girls' high school, an establishment bearing the name of a great man of letters, they were happy. As a result, my father-in-law did not press the point when I civilly told him that I had done all I could in marrying Jude, and as for anything else, it was better to leave me to literature.

Jude was the youngest of six, and the other five siblings had provided their father with more descendants than anyone else he knew: thirty grandchildren. Or maybe thirty-two;

I didn't count them. My father-in-law left Jude and me alone, and did not mention babies again. In a more religious family, Jude would have taken holy orders. In a sense, I took the place of Jude's sacred calling.

Was the absence of physical contact between us natural? On our wedding night, I had picked up a book instead of undressing and giving myself up to amorous play. Jude had made no comment, but spent a long time in the bathroom and was asleep before I had finished my chapter. On the evenings that followed, Jude prepared for bed in the most normal way imaginable, without showing the slightest sign of frustration. We were husband and wife, and that seemed to be enough. I hoped so, for I was incapable of touching or being touched by my partner. The mere idea terrified me, and I was grateful to be spared that trial. I cannot say that Jude's body disgusted me; it inspired no feeling in me, neither desire nor revulsion. My pleasures were of a different kind. But what about Jude's?

Without monopolizing the bathroom, Jude carried out a little ritual every evening. Whatever happened, however late we went to bed, even at Christmas, Jude's underwear had to be washed in the bathroom sink. Why this habit? No one had inculcated it into me. I had never seen anyone else do such a thing, not my mother or my sisters and, of course, no man. We left my mother to deal with the laundry. I told myself that this little ceremony was peculiar to Jude, performed out of a personal regard for privacy, and in order to remove any taint of bodily secretions and start the new day afresh. My mother-in-law employed a washerwoman, and in adolescence Jude's natural modesty probably dictated this means of warding off any indiscreet revelations by a servant.

We never discussed the ritual, I never asked the reason for it, we simply did not talk about it. Jude and I had our own lives, which came together at the end of the day. We spent our evenings side by side, neither of us showing great interest in the other. We were a married couple. We had sworn fidelity and mutual support, but who said anything about love, about enriching one another's experience by the mutual exploration of our bodies? No doubt Jude had an inner life — who doesn't? — but I never went to the trouble of discovering it. I preferred to relish the rapid disintegration of Gregor Samsa, to watch Hans Castorp's slow death agonies at the foot of his magic mountain, or to join Mrs C. as she came to the end of her twenty-four hours in the life of a woman.

Did Jude make love alone? I can consider that question today; at the time it never occurred to me. Was the ceremonial purification of undergarments a substitute for physical contact with a body that my spouse desired? I have no idea if Jude indulged in solitary pleasures in my absence, stimulating the arousal that I did not provide. Did those manicured fingers touch and stroke in simulation of someone else's hands, my hands?

I may appear to have devoted my whole life to the asceticism of literature, but I have allowed myself a fair share of pleasure. Coming up from the cellar at night during the war, particularly when the cold had forced me to abandon a book, I sometimes let loose too violent desires, an irrepressible longing for I don't know exactly what sensual experience, in a few movements carried out under the rough sheets that my mother must have gotten from a convent; an aunt of hers had been Mother Superior of some obscure order.

Meanwhile Jude snored beside me, and in my mind I immersed myself in *Death in Venice*, thinking of the silhouette of the adolescent trailed by Gustav von Aschenbach through the alleyways of the Serenissima. I imagined the boy with his almond eyes, the pale flesh of his arms, his smooth, hairless thighs, powerful beneath his skin. Was what I saw young Tadzio, or the memory of my friend who once read to me from Thomas Mann on the third floor of a student dorm at the time of the Weimar Republic? Half asleep, I shaped the features of a new hero, part Hans-Joachim and part someone else, like the statue on one of those public buildings constructed shortly before the war, the Palace of Justice, the Public Baths, a figure with a firm chin, a determined eye, jutting pectorals.

Often, however, the obsessive memory of my sister's orgasms, the shaking of the drawing-room chandelier which I had been obliged to endure that very day, prevented me for a time from reaching a climax, conflicting as it did with the grace of that fugitive creature as it passed across the canopy of my bed, Thomas Mann's character merged with the friend of my youth. The phrases from *Death in Venice,* the youthful voice of Hans-Joachim, finally won the day and gave me relief. "To behold this living figure, lovely and austere in its early masculinity, with dripping locks and beautiful as a young god, approaching out of the depths of the sky and the sea, rising and escaping from the elements."

3

THE OCCUPATION and all the commitments that came with it soon caught up with me. At first I had been like many of my compatriots. I had watched, open-mouthed, as the German troops goose-stepped down the main street of our town, their conquering step pounding the soil of our native land. I disliked their arrogant bearing, just as later I would dislike Volker's wholehearted, uncomplicated virility. I imagined his prick enormous, powerful, out of all proportion with reality, but how could he give my sister Anne so much pleasure except with an organ of exceptional dimensions and stamina?

I also disliked the ease with which France knuckled under to the hereditary foe. Here the local paper had outdone itself.

To read it on May 13, 1940, you would have thought that the French army was victorious in the Ardennes. On June 24 we learned that the armistice had been signed at Rethondes, and three days later the newspaper was paying tribute to yesterday's enemy. What choice did it have? What had I myself done to resist the occupying power? During what we called the Phony War, before much actual fighting took place in Europe, the army general staff had called on my knowledge of German to translate information published by the Nazi press. A young, baby-faced soldier would bring me a stack of documents late in the afternoon when I came back from school. He had a military haircut, a close-fitting tunic, piercing blue eyes, and muscles standing out just beneath the skin. I read through the papers and translated only the passages that struck me as significant. The soldier waited patiently on a chair outside my study door. He hummed Chopin nocturnes in a deep, warm voice. He had asked me, in a heavy foreign accent, if his humming disturbed me. I said: On the contrary, I like the tunes. I wanted to add: I like your voice, too.

The young man soothed me as I read those venomous columns about the enemies of the German people, always the same, the British, the French, the Jews. As I went through the pages of German, I came across many horrors and much hatred, amounting to almost constant incitement to commit murder. The Jews in particular were vilified. The Nazis wanted them eliminated from the German people as if they were a tumor to be cut out. The speeches I had to translate

were full of obscene allusions. You would have thought that
the unfortunate women of Germany risked rape at every
moment in the streets of Munich and Weimar, for to the
National Socialist mind Jews were always on the prowl, apparently with the sole aim of despoiling Gretchen's virtue.
Synagogues were dens of vice, brothels where young German girls might be held captive. Nazi morality had forbidden the marriage of Aryans and Jews, and indeed prohibited
any sexual relationship between them. Had they stationed a
policeman under every bed to make sure no one broke the
law? If Jude had been Jewish, if we had lived in Germany,
would we have had to show proof of virginity to avoid the
risk of imprisonment? We wouldn't have had any problems
there.

I don't like the word *Aryan*, I never did. It means nothing, it
is a word good for nothing but making trouble. But how did
you say so?

When I had finished my pages of translation, I did not always get up from my desk at once. I would stay there, pen in
my fingers, my gaze straying over the flowers on the wall-
paper, my heart going out to the boy's musical murmuring. I
let it take me over. After a while my body would move, as if
sleepwalking, toward the young man. I put down my pen, I
stood up, I opened the door, and at once he was on his feet,

standing at attention. Several times, as I gave him the package of newspapers and my translations, I wanted to unbutton his impeccably ironed tunic, but I always restrained my desire. It was forbidden.

Then the armistice was signed. I realized that the young soldier would not be coming anymore; I didn't even know his first name. I cherished the memory of his youthful face, his nipples showing under his army tunic on very cold days (or did I arouse some kind of desire in him?), his deep voice distilling whole and eighth notes. I continued to teach at the school but had given up private tutorial work since my marriage. I became accustomed to the Occupation, to the unoccupied zone (it did not stay unoccupied for long), to ration coupons. Jude and I were allowed two hundred fifty grams of bread a day, two hundred grams of meat a week (although we were not in the same category, since men had larger rations than women). We got used to air raids and nights spent in the shelters, which were our cellars. In our part of town all the houses had cellars, so we were not obliged to take neighbors in. There were four of us, my mother, my sister, Jude and I; the wine cellar was large enough and my reading room was spared.

I watched the occupying forces march past in uniform carrying swastika banners; I often passed the *Soldaten-kino,* the German soldiers' cinema. I fled the house at the approach of Volker; I could not imagine doing anything at all to oppose this encroaching invader. The Resistance was organizing itself, but it was nothing to do with me: I was neither a Jew nor a Communist. As for my patriotism, it was like many other people's: lukewarm. I hated Volker and the sound of his heels on the steps of the walnut staircase that four generations of my forebears had trodden. I could have killed him on one of those days when he came to pour his seed into my sister, I could have buried him down in the cellar under my secret library and no one would have known anything about it. My fingernails would have been rather black when I came up again, but I'd have scrubbed them before sitting down to dinner.

However, my sister would have been anxious. She'd have ended up in Ravensbrück or some military brothel on the Russian front. She'd have spent her days on a pallet, thighs spread, with the youth of Germany screwing her, no more than two minutes per soldier, they didn't have all day, that included Hans-Joachim, the friend of my youth, he must be somewhere at the front. I didn't think I could contribute to the struggle against the occupying forces in that way, but if all the young people of my generation had killed the Germans who came to make love to their sisters, if all the young girls of good family had snatched up kitchen knives to cut the throats of all those Volkers with their neatly shaven necks, we'd have been rid of the German Reich's army in no time at all.

I submerged myself in daily life. Shops changed hands. Madame Bloch's draper's shop and the À l'Émeraude jeweler's shop kept by old Mademoiselle Dreyfus had been taken over by rivals keen on the celebratory nationalist atmosphere. We didn't know what had become of the former owners, they had disappeared, the gardens of their houses were invaded by weeds, the shutters were closed. Were they hiding behind them? Or had they taken refuge with friends elsewhere? Had they reached Switzerland, where, as the press liked to claim, they were living on money they had made at the expense of good Frenchmen and Frenchwomen? Who was to be believed?

Now and then the Germans came to pick up students coming out of school. I had watched such a scene more than once, for the windows of my classroom looked out on the entrance to the boys' high school. Dutilleul, Marcellin, Garabédian, Proust — I hadn't known they were in the Resistance, but they had been taken away and didn't come back. I had pretended to notice nothing, despite the pistol shots, and little Lachman, whom I'd known since he was only so high, who began running and was shot down in the middle of the street. When the shots were fired, when Lachman fell to the ground, my students had their noses in their exercise books, and I was reading aloud.

Der du von dem Himmel bist
Alles Leid und Schmerzen stillest,
Den, der doppelt elend ist,
Doppelt mit Erquickung füllest.

How lovely the language of Goethe and Goebbels was. Lachman's parents lived not far from our house. We didn't go to see them after the tragedy. It was out of the question for my sister, who had her official standing to consider, but what about my mother and me? I think we were simply afraid that their misfortune would affect us, we would be seen going to offer our condolences to the parents of a member of the Resistance. And a Jew at that.

I didn't like it when certain authors were banned. Childhood acquaintances of mine went underground, the young men to avoid compulsory labor service, while girls, for love of their fiancés or their country, started cycling round the French countryside, their bicycle frames laden with coded messages for the Resistance. Personally I couldn't do without Thomas Mann; that was my threshold of tolerance where the occupying power was concerned. And I organized my own little underground trafficking, a mercenary without a gun.

It happened one morning. The occupier had been occupying us for some time now. I was giving the tenth-grade students a lesson on the use of the genitive case after the preposition *während*. There was a knock on the classroom door. The headmaster Muller came in, an Alsatian of the 1940 exodus who had replaced Valabrègue when he was dismissed by the

Vichy government. The headmaster was closely followed by two Germans in Gestapo uniform. The taller — fair-haired, red-cheeked, with an aggressively jutting jaw — addressed me in German, telling me to follow them. I said: Ladies, please excuse me. I stowed my notes inside my briefcase, put on my Prince of Wales check coat with its rabbit-fur collar, and followed the two men under the gaze of the headmaster, who looked vaguely sorry for me.

The Gestapo occupied one of the finest buildings in town, the Hôtel des Barres, formerly the headquarters of a regional bank. Since the beginning of the Occupation the pavements around the building, once very busy because they led from one shopping street to another, had been deserted, as if people were afraid to come too close to that alarming address, 10, place du Maréchal-Pétain. After the war it became the Chamber of Commerce, and the address was 10, place du Général-de-Gaulle. We went a long way round rather than pass the walls of the Gestapo building and risk looking through one of its windows, in a moment of irresistible curiosity, to see something we would rather not have witnessed. It was known that the vaults of the bank down in the basement had been turned into cells, and they were not good places to be. In speaking of the building we called it Les Barres: little Bergeron has been taken off to Les Barres. Those summoned to the building went in through the big front door, and often came out by the back door in a canvas-covered truck bound for some unknown destination.

I didn't know why I had been summoned, but I was very

much afraid of never coming out at the front again. I wasn't Jewish, I had never had any contact with the Resistance (my guarded conduct toward Lachman's parents was not the only precaution I took), I had scrupulously observed the curfew, and who could know about my secret library? On the way, I could have started running like Lachman to give my escort the slip. I had a slim chance of escaping the bullets of their machine guns. But why would I do that? I was guilty of almost nothing.

The few hundred yards separating my classroom from the Gestapo offices were interminable. I was walking with three uniformed Germans, I avoided the eyes of passersby, fearing to see a familiar face; everyone in town knew me, or almost everyone. It would be only a few hours before public rumor made me a victim of this filthy war, and one of its heroic characters, too. Suddenly I would be featured as one of those hotheads who were arrested for rising against the Boche. I was terrified of what awaited me in the Gestapo building, but I felt a certain pride in assuming this accidental identity as the sight of me aroused looks of alarm and admiration. I was thinking what I would have to say to show that my conduct had been irreproachable. Would I have to prove my tractability? It was one thing to have failed to do or say anything against the occupying forces, to leave my bike in the garage while others set off on theirs for the underground, quite another to boast of it to the enemy in order to save my skin. "I didn't do a thing, Monsieur Head of the Gestapo, sir, I let your army occupy every last square inch of our country without batting an eyelid, I swear it." Was I capable of that?

We had passed the gate of the building. I climbed the monumental staircase leading to the second floor. I remembered climbing it once before with my father and sisters on the day when we came to draw out the money, quite a tidy sum, that my grandmother had left the family when she died. That was in the days when the building was a bank. Now I was told to sit in a chair outside the double doors of the manager's office, a magnificent example of the joiner's craft, with gilded molding that dated from the Louis XIV period. I waited for an eternity. No one thought of bringing me anything to eat. When evening came — it was winter and night fell early, but all the same I had waited the whole afternoon — I was finally let into the office. I found myself facing the local Gestapo commandant, a courteous and resolute man. My professional skills had caught up with me. I was told to make myself available to the occupying forces for various jobs of translation and interpreting, nothing onerous, only a few hours a week. A minuscule act of collaboration, in fact, not to be compared with my former brother-in-law's membership in the Legion of French Volunteers. Why call on my services so late, when the Allies had already landed in North Africa? Did I have the option of refusing? I dared not ask; there would be time to think about that once I was home.

The commandant had spoken to me in German. I felt a certain wish to reply in French, to indicate to him and persuade myself that I was not forgetting my country, but I dared not. Out of discretion, timidity, fear? I was afraid of going out by the back door in a canvas-covered truck. And replying in German was a reflex, too, like second nature, I so much enjoyed speaking the language. As the smoker rediscovers the sensation of smoke lacerating his larynx, I liked to feel its sounds passing through my throat like a horde of wild horses, particularly the sounds that don't exist in French: *Ich habe das nie getan, ich möchte doch etwas machen* — I could pronounce that perfectly.

So I came through the front gate in the other direction, giving the passersby not a glance. A few hours later, rumor would say I was one of the few who had managed to return unscathed from a Gestapo summons. People would wonder how I'd managed to slip through the net. They would make connections with raids to pick up Resistance members at dawn the next day, or the arrest of one of my colleagues at the school, and they'd tell themselves I must have dropped a few names, or else how did I manage to come out of Les Barres through the main entrance?

In order to silence this rumor, I had to disclose a few scraps of the truth, which I would rather have kept to myself, for I didn't refuse my services to the Gestapo commandant, neither when I was first summoned nor on any later occasion. I said I had no real choice, it was that or the canvas-covered truck. I even said the commandant had threatened to arrest my mother and my sister, despite her status as a collaborator's widow, and send them who knows where, maybe to a brothel for Vichyist légionnaires in Sidi Bel Abbès, or somewhere else now that the Allies had recaptured Algeria. It wasn't true; the commandant had made no threats. He had spoken respectfully to me. I even felt that he was showing me a certain respect. He didn't say anything about it, but he seemed to admire my command of his language.

His consideration went no further than that. I did not have a messenger bring material to my home, as in the days of the French army. I went to collect my reading matter once a week. I sometimes had to wait a long time before Herr des Roulieres, a man of Huguenot descent whose name was pronounced with an accent but written without one, saw me and gave me the pages I was to translate. There was no deference from him. His was a dry and very Teutonic manner, despite his origins. Was he avenging the fate inflicted on his ancestors by the eldest daughter of the Church, centuries after the event?

On leaving the office of Herr des Roulieres, I would come out through the front entrance again, past the monumental barred gate, which claimed to be like the gate of Versailles. I sometimes felt like forgetting the engagement, but I was always perfectly punctual. I was ashamed to be serving the Gestapo, I hated to see the Boche shamelessly hoisting the emblems of the Third Reich beneath the architectural masterpieces of the Grand Siècle. However, I never allowed myself to be a minute late, even if I knew I would have to wait for Herr des Roulieres, sometimes for several hours. My punctuality was my pride, my way of resisting — a very circumspect way, I admit. I waited patiently on a wooden chair in the corridor, and it was a real trial, for I saw far too many people pass that way, all kinds of offenders against Teutonic law and order: young people who felt none of my own weakness, or those condemned by their birth, Jews rooted out from God knows where, gypsies arrested by the caravanful.

I hated these long waits. I pretended not to know why, I pretended it was only the humiliation of having to serve the occupying power, but of course there was something else: my eyes saw so many people going up and down that corridor, their outlines were impressed on my retina, the colors of their coats, their faces. And the more such images as these were superimposed on my mind, the harder it was for me to say I didn't know anything about it: abusive detentions, beatings, torture, imprisonment, summary executions, people sent somewhere miles away, families who wouldn't be separated. And what could I do but stay there, planted in that chair, waiting at Herr des Roulieres's pleasure (he would be late coming out just to humiliate me a little more — I saw no other reason for a descendant of the Huguenots to be late).

I did not ask myself questions then, which surprises me today. How do you find yourself with a grenade in your hand, blowing up a railway line or emptying your magazine into a patrol of men in battle-gray uniforms? Does it take courage, recklessness, or simply a desire to get out of the routine of a predictable life? Monsieur, I immersed myself in the German language to read Goethe, Heine, the Mann brothers, not to watch you send adolescents to the firing squad. That's why I shall not translate anything for you. Or I could have walked out of the office in a courteous manner, without saying anything to the commandant; I could have taken the tram from the Hôtel-des-Barres stop to the terminal, then the funicular railway to the Roche-Noire plateau, and I could have disappeared to join the Resistance. Then again, I could have pretended to have an attack of hay fever and blown my nose, in front of the Gestapo men on duty, on one of those red-and-white banners adorned with enormous swastikas like the branded backsides of cattle in westerns, those morbid banners that were draped from the balcony of the Hôtel des Barres down both sides of the outside steps, disfiguring its facade.

Instead, I went home. Was I afraid of death, cold, lack of privacy, hunger? Was it the idea of "going underground" that upset me, the feeling that to some extent I would be lost from sight, would lose my very existence there? I didn't know it, but people lived a double life in the Resistance: they had two names, two identities, sometimes two faces, almost two bodies. The women there wore men's caps and trousers. Wasn't this a chance to be someone else, change your skin, your hairstyle and color, your sex, the company you kept?

I didn't want any of that. I felt reasonably all right as I

was, I was happy enough with my eyes and face and body, and was I really so upset by my sister Anne's small or large compromises? What was I if I was no longer a teacher of German? I couldn't take refuge in conjugal life. The only friend I'd ever had was a German. Above all, I wanted to be left to read in peace. My nights in the cellar were enough for me. I might translate a few pages a week, a propaganda pamphlet here, the Obergruppenführer's speech there, but *Death in Venice* was worth it. I wouldn't have my library with me up there in the mountains. And how could I read my favorite authors in the original in the middle of a Resistance hideout, when the aim was to eliminate as many Germans as possible, making chalk marks side by side on the wall to keep a record of the body count? Chalk soils your hands, its squeak on the blackboard is excruciating, but I could tolerate those inconveniences when the purpose was to copy out a verse by Heine or Schiller.

Des Roulieres's office was on the ground floor; you passed it to reach the cellars, the former vault where the safes must have been replaced by torture chambers. As the weeks went by, I came to understand the bustle and confusion of the Nazis' activities. Political prisoners were sent down to the basement. I often heard howls. I blanched, but the Germans continued their comings and goings before my eyes as if nothing was the matter, as if men and women, often hardly out of childhood, were not being slaughtered on the floor below. The Jews and gypsies (there were fewer of those) disappeared down the end of my corridor and were assembled in a room with no windows which had been the bank cashier's office. The glazed door with the grilled panel over it had been taken away and replaced by a metal door.

I saw whole families pass by, father, mother, daughters, grandmother, men on their own, even children without parents. Often I didn't know the prisoners. They must have been Parisian Jews who had come to hide in this region. They had been flushed out of an attic, a convent's kitchen quarters, or, if they were children, from a Catholic family who had fostered them. Everyone knew that the region was full of Jews. I heard some of them speaking standard German, others a kind of German which I took to be the Berlin dialect, or something like it. They spoke Spanish, Hungarian, Czech, Arabic, and French, too, with all kinds of different accents. I even heard some speaking ordinary French, but those were very often people I knew. They were our own Jews, they had been part of my landscape since childhood. I felt rather uncomfortable when their coats brushed past my shoes.

There was Dr. Astruc, a pretentious man I didn't like, and Kahn, proprietor of the Excelsior cinema, a self-made man who put on aristocratic airs, with his wife and their twin daughters. One morning I saw Madame Bloch the draper. Where had she been hiding all these months? When I used to go to her shop with my mother, she would wax ecstatic over my blue eyes, and would give me barley sugar and a big kiss on my left cheek. She would hug me in her good-natured way. I liked her warmth, her cinnamon perfume — I wanted to smell the same — and I liked the odor of mercerized cotton and mothballs in her shop. My mother did not approve of these excesses from a shopkeeper. She would have preferred that I avoid these kisses, but Madame Bloch gave me the physical contact I did not get at home. I happily buried my face in her soft throat, I kept the mark of her lipstick on my cheek and the trace of her perfume on my coat collar as long as possible.

I was waiting patiently outside des Roulieres's office when the door at the end of the corridor opened noisily and the plump little woman appeared, neat as a new pin, face made up, wearing a hat and almost extinguished by a thick black fur coat with glints of red in it. There were two German soldiers with her, one on each side, and she walked with a firm step, like someone who knew what was what. She came closer, and I feared she might recognize me. All the time she was walking past me I wished the floor would open and swallow me up. I examined my nails, which were immaculate, as usual. She didn't notice me, or perhaps she didn't recognize me, for I had grown. The soldiers shut her up in the cashier's office. I prayed that she would stay there until I had left the place. A few minutes later des Roulieres saved my life by opening his office door.

I found all sorts of excuses to stay with des Roulieres as long as possible. Suddenly I was well disposed, almost cordial, toward this officer whom I disliked and who showed me little courtesy, merely to keep myself from coming face-to-face with Madame Bloch. I tried to leave his office by the other door; I don't know where it went, but at least not into the corridor I wanted to avoid. The attempt failed. Des Roulieres barred my way and firmly indicated the usual door. Luckily there was no one in the corridor. I left without more ado. Afterwards I often thought of Madame Bloch. She did not come back, she had vanished. After the war no one mentioned her. Her shop was still called The Thimble, but it was kept by an Italian lady with a moustache. Later it became a shoe shop and then a bank with a vault in the basement, but no torture chamber.

The war went on, and no one really knew who was going to win. The press told lies, perhaps Radio London told lies, or perhaps it sometimes told the truth, but how could we know? We were busy with all sorts of things. I translated, I read, I went down to the cellar as often as possible, I taught, I kept my weekly appointment, the guards with their swastika badges clicked their heels as I passed, I was part of the Gestapo furniture. I would have liked to veil my face on entering the building, not so much to disappear as to not see anything. Resistance fighters? Jews? *Dis est-ce que t'as vu Monte Carlo?* people sang. *Non, j'ai vu monter personne.* Saw nothing, heard nothing. Shadows slipped past me in the corridor outside des Roulieres's office, every man, every woman was like a plane tree lining a road. From my seat in the bus I saw them pass out of the corner of my eye, but I was looking elsewhere, straight ahead. I couldn't even take refuge in examining the blue line of the Vosges mountains, my eyes stared into the mist rising from the ground on winter mornings, I mustn't raise them and risk seeing faces.

It's the landscape that counts, isn't that right? Well, the landscape's there, the one my ancestors have seen for centuries, spruce forests, high-altitude lakes, the snowy mountain peaks in winter. Men and women pass. They run toward their fate. Before you have time to draw breath, they're gone, swallowed up by the passage of time. They leave no trace behind in this world. Some die at a ripe old age, others earlier. It's like birth, you don't choose the hour of your arrival or your departure. There have always been wars, injustice, victims, executioners. Madame Bloch was over fifty when I last saw her in the corridor; she would be dead now, no one has ever been known to live to a hundred and twenty. People drop off the perch some time or other and drag you down with them.

Literature keeps them in their places. I did not want to fall. Was that why I liked to read so much? So that I could find people just where I had left them, catch them by the sleeve to prevent them from disappearing, so that I could keep my balance, standing with my two feet planted firmly on the ground? I still had whole libraries to read.

⅏⅏⅏

One day I saw the soldier again, the one who used to bring me my allotted translations at home during the Phony War. There he was, right in front of me. The front door opened and a group was pushed in: Jews. It was obvious. They were not like the others, although I can't say exactly how I recognized them. The young man was in civilian clothes, taller than the others, imposing. He dominated them. I knew him again at once.

Almost two years had passed since he last visited me. Two years of the Occupation, of humiliation, of sacrifices and little compromises of principle, two years of waiting outside des Roulieres's office and vainly attempting not to recognize any of the faces going down the corridor. Pages and pages translated for the occupying forces had nearly erased that earlier time when I heard his voice humming nocturnes on the other side of my door. My life as a palimpsest: an ill-intentioned scribe had scratched out one story to write another over it, and the first was now indecipherable.

Where had he been since the armistice? Sent home? A prisoner in Germany? I had often dreamed of him. Naked, standing at attention, holding my translation in his hands at the level of the pubis. In the dream my fingers ran over the hollow of his shoulder, his breast, as firm as a horse's cheek, his belly, my forefinger turned, turned at the side of the hollow, my finger in his navel, my nail, filed to a point, scratching his slightly grainy skin, the caress going further to lose

itself in his hips and buttocks. The soldier stood at attention, captain's orders, despite his nakedness and my caresses,
only a slight quiver of the lip, despite defeat and the Occupation. That was in my dreams.

I'd never expected to see him again, and here he was in
the middle of the Gestapo corridor, just as I was expecting
des Roulieres. In that brightly lit corridor, his face was not as
I remembered it. The man did not see me. He had aged, or
rather matured, no doubt as a result of those two years of
war, which surely counted double. He no longer looked like
a child made to put on a uniform too young. His cheeks
were hollow, but he was still impressive with his height and
his distinguished profile. This war had given his gaze a pride
that I did not remember in him. I kept watching him; he
did not see me, his gaze was lost somewhere else, the other
Jews no longer existed around him. He was alone in the
middle of the corridor, brought there by fate.

4

IT WASN'T EASY in the cellar at first. I hadn't expected to be hiding anyone there. Herman (that was the ex-soldier's name) had no change of clothing. He had to sleep on the floor for the first few days, since there was no bed. The sanitary arrangements were the worst part. He had to give me his chamber pot to empty, and he felt ashamed. I didn't like it too much myself, but what choice did we have? Today, that physical modesty makes me smile; a chamber pot is nothing, just a lingering bad smell, people have done much worse things since, eating their neighbors in a wrecked aircraft on the Andes Cordillera, drinking piss in a cattle car. All I did was empty shit during the war.

I don't remember exactly how he made it to the cellar. It

all happened so fast; the images didn't imprint themselves on my mind's eye. It was a combination of circumstances: an SS man with his back turned, the clerk whose job it was to register the names of new arrivals taking his lunch break. I vaguely remember that we walked out of the Hôtel des Barres through the main entrance, the sentries clicked their heels, and I couldn't find it in me to laugh at that comical scene. And then, who knows, perhaps a Gestapo man turned a blind eye at a timely moment, covering our escape because he liked the look of Herman or the small of my back. In those days human lives could depend on such chances, such ridiculous weaknesses and tiny acts of disobedience.

I took Herman home. My mother was out shopping, my sister was up on the second floor, where she could hardly even be said to be dishonoring the family anymore. Only the big mirror in the hall saw us pass, and mirrors have no memory, secrets slip over the glass leaving no trace. I left Herman in the cellar and hurried back to the Gestapo building. I had to go back there to get the translations. It was very dangerous: what had happened after our flight? Had they realized that there was one Jew missing? Had the sentries reported our escape?

I feverishly climbed the staircase of the Hôtel des Barres. Inside, the crowd of Jews had been absorbed, the corridor was empty. They must have been shut up in the former cashier's office, unless they had been taken out through the back door and loaded into trucks. Des Roulieres was pleased to have caught me out: I was late. I didn't offer any apologies but picked up the bundle of documents he had thrown down on the desk with the contempt of the victor, and I left his office. I was going to war, and it felt good. I was resisting, I was saving a man, and what a man! I was half dead with fear but my life was beginning to make sense. I could put up with des Roulieres's humiliation of me, the way the sentries clicked their heels wouldn't be like a slap in the face anymore, I could look the victims in the eye. The boy with the turquoise gaze at the back of the cellar was saving my life. I was beginning to resist in my own tiny way.

I was very lucky, now that I think of it. The Nazis hadn't realized that Herman was missing and the other Jews told no tales, although people said Jews were cowards. Perhaps their cowardice kept them quiet.

I went on with my laborious gleaning, but it wasn't books I took down to my underground retreat now. When I came back from school I went scavenging for old things that had been thrown out with the garbage, and there weren't many of those in the war. These days we throw away, throw away, throw away, throwing away has become an activity in itself, but back then the world spent its time mending, darning, recycling, even re-serving leftover food.

You unraveled knitted garments. I would stand motionless, my arms a foot apart, while my mother wound wool around my hands as she pulled at a steadily unraveling cardigan. When she had made the skein, she dipped it in water to straighten out the wool so that she could knit it again. The sweater I had worn when I was fifteen made at least four tops for my sister Isabelle's children. And when I couldn't offer the use of my hands because I had homework to do, or later when my mother didn't like to ask me because I was grown up, she used the back of a dining chair, but it wasn't as good. My sister Anne could never stay still for more than two minutes on end, so my mother soon realized that it was a waste of time to use her.

We had to make the cellar more comfortable, but wartime garbage bins were almost as empty as wartime plates. It was out of the question to bring a mattress down; my own strength would never be enough, and I couldn't take anyone into my confidence. So I collected rags, odds and ends of wool, bits of straw, and we sewed one by night down in the cellar. Herman was a tailor. That is to say, he was much more than that, but he'd been good with a needle since childhood. I would never have thought his big hands capable of such precise work when they held a piece of fabric.

We spent whole nights sewing. He used long lengths of thread, put small stitches into the pieces of fabric to be joined together, and then pulled the threads through without ever getting them tangled. He could easily pierce the thickest fabric with a firm little thrust. I sat beside him, my hands holding another part of the work, toiling away over a few stitches covering just a few irregular inches, while he was producing several yards of impeccable needlework.

I brought pieces of material salvaged from here and there, and we added them to what we had already done.

"How about this dishcloth next to that bit of old sheet?"

"I'd put it here, going on from the beige stuff."

We talked in the dim light as we sewed. He asked me about the books I had read, I answered him. He told me about the books he knew himself. He asked the questions; he did the talking. From time to time our conversation died away. Sometimes he began humming. His warm voice surrounded me, just as it had during the Phony War. We often sewed in silence by the light of the little reading lamp. We concentrated on our work, he in particular, because I kept glancing surreptitiously at him. I liked to see him.

As I went down to the cellar, I passed my mother's Singer sewing machine. Our work would have gone faster if we could have used it, but it would have deprived me of those nights when I liked to watch Herman the tailor's fingers dancing.

We were proud of the mattress we had made for him out of nothing. The sheets were like those maps of France that hung on the walls of primary schools showing the regions in different colors. We'd call it patchwork today, I think — a strange kind of geography that was ours alone. I stole two shirts from my father's wardrobe. My mother never opened it now, and if he came home from POW camp, would he remember just how many shirts he'd left there before the war? I presented Herman with a set of my old underwear and a set of Jude's. I liked to think of him clad alternately in men's and women's undergarments beneath his trousers; it was a mild way of humiliating him. Blame it on the war, but I wanted to maintain a certain ascendancy over him, make his life easier but not too easy, in the same way as you might keep a canary in a cage and pretend you've forgotten to change its water just so that it can't bathe properly. I could have done much worse, for he was at my mercy. I could throw him out of the cellar anytime I liked, send him back into the open and leave him to the dogs.

If Herman was to survive he had to stay in the cellar. I had captured him, and that was easy enough, because he had willingly fallen into step with me to escape the Gestapo. I didn't have to make any great effort to keep him: circumstances themselves kept him under my thumb. But I'm exaggerating; I didn't take advantage of the situation. It's only now that I realize what power I had then.

Herman spelled his name with a single *n;* he insisted on

that. It took me a long time to accept the spelling. I saw it as
a German first name, but many Jews in Poland were called
Herman, and Herman was a Jew. I had never been so close
to one, apart from Madame Bloch for one of her occasional
soft, perfumed kisses.

My favorite Hermann before him was Hermann Hesse, par-
ticularly his *Steppenwolf.* That title had stayed in my official
library up on the second floor. I found the book again, with
Herman in mind. I had almost forgotten it, in between *The
Sorrows of Young Werther* and Kleist's *The Prince of Homburg.*
As I said, I was avoiding officially approved literature.
Thomas Mann had come to fill my life. I took Hermann out
of my library again and gave him space on my bedside table.
When I was up on the second floor, with Jude beside me, I
would think of Herman down in the cellar, and I consoled
myself with Hesse. In this way, I spent the whole evening
with Hermann, even if he had to be spelled with a double *n,*
as a way of bringing our secret life out into the open.

I said that Herman was at my mercy, but wasn't it the other
way around? The troubled state into which the young soldier had cast me during the Phony War was revived as soon
as he began living in the cellar. I loved the man. The dim
light down there hid him from me and increased my desire,

just as the darkness makes an amusement park ghost train exciting. But what about him? He was grateful to me for saving him; would that be enough to win him over? Would he touch me one night?

I can't think now how Herman managed to stay down in the cellar so long. Two years, three months and two weeks, while I emptied the chamber pot twice a day. And no one noticed anything. Well, maybe Jude did, but I will never know. The destined partner of my life — we had been close without ever touching — committed suicide on February 8, 1944. I did not know why. Jude left no farewell note.

Coming up from the cellar one night I found a naked, motionless body lying on its stomach in the marital bed, in a pool of blood. The corpse's buttocks were upward, and I saw them for the first time. I know that may seem incredible, but it is the truth, I swear. I had lost nothing by failing to undress Jude, whose buttocks were not beautiful; they aroused no desire in me, spread there limp between back and thighs, with a sparse but disturbing growth of hair emerging from the anus. Or perhaps the circumstances, such a macabre discovery made on my return from the cellar, had destroyed any capacity in me to desire them.

I did feel a vague wish to kiss Jude; for the first time that would have been a sincere gesture, but it was too late now. Jude did not deserve such an insult. In the bathroom I found underclothes recently wrung out and drying on the towel rail. What despair had deprived the quiet, withdrawn Jude of any wish to live? I had done nothing to help my partner open up and blossom, yet it had been my duty to do so. On the contrary, I had left Jude immured in solitude, and I had deliberately avoided imagining the frustration of living with such a marriage. I have not been perfectly truthful. I said that Jude never tried to approach me, but I had made sure no such approach was ever made. Is sitting immersed in a German book any way to spend your wedding night? Jude's body did not attract me, so I did all I could to keep my distance and avoid all contact with it.

Was that naked body, which I found after the life was out of it, a body daubed with blood so dark it was almost black, Jude's only posthumous message, a message of mourning never touched by any erotic life between us? Was this suicide a way of drawing the final line, a present that Jude was giving me, allowing me to devote myself entirely to saving Herman?

That suicide in the middle of the war was in rather bad taste. Jude's life could have been sacrificed to better effect in resisting the occupying power, for instance by staging an operation to blow up the municipal theater during a recital by Charles Trenet for an audience of German soldiers and Milice paramilitaries. We had lived through over two years of the Occupation side by side as man and wife (why is the phrase always in that order, never "wife and man"?) and I had no idea of Jude's opinion on the subject of the Occupation and the Resistance. We didn't discuss it, we didn't discuss anything, not even those underclothes drying on the rack, indeed particularly not the underclothes. I merely registered that they were there when I went into the bathroom. I didn't deduce anything from their presence. They spoiled the look of the room, a constant reproach, a flag at half-mast, rather like the inscription "Air-Raid Shelter to Hold 50 Persons" which could be seen on the apartment buildings on the avenue de la République until the 1970s. The insurance company that owned them gutted the air-raid shelters when they renovated the facades. But I still have my own personal air-raid shelter, as a feeling deep inside me, and I have Jude's suicide on my conscience, or on some small part of it.

Why do I feel guilty of that sin? I have lived with it for almost sixty years now. I was not cut out to be a janissary, to stand guard over Jude's life. We had been the two principals in the drama of our marriage, a tale of a couple who shared the same bed for eight years without ever touching each other, who ate breakfast at the same table without ever talking to one another. When our parents suggested the marriage I said, *Pourquoi pas?* It reminded me of Commander Charcot's ship — my father had told me of his Antarctic exploits when I was a child — but Jude didn't say no either, or make any conditions. A marriage contract was surely all that was wanted? If I had been told that Jude expected something more of our union, sex, conversation, I would not have agreed to the marriage, I would have offered free German tuition for years on end if that would have extricated me elegantly from my predicament. *Ich bin du bist er ist,* let's be just good friends, *Ich weiss nicht was soll es bedeuten dass ich so traurig bin,* we won't mention the matter again.

I neither loved nor desired Jude, and I don't remember having felt that there was the slightest love or any desire for sexual relations on Jude's part either. Nothing. Our relationship was a tranquil plain, a landscape without irregular features or gusts of wind, ordinary and everyday. But *sans souci,* without care, like Frederick the Great's palace. Nothing. That was the word for it, the word that Louis XVI wrote in his journal for July 14, 1789. Nothing. And the next day nothing. And the same the day after that.

So why this suicide, with no reason given for it, no explanation? Just to make me feel the guilt I hadn't felt before? I can't answer that question. If Jude wanted to make love so much, to touch and be touched, why not take the initiative and ignore my reluctance? Conjugal rape, for instance. Apparently it happens quite often, and it would have been less violent than this murderous act. Jude's suicide remains an enigma, and it weighs on my mind. Our marriage was already a mystery, but that did not trouble me. I adjusted to it. Only later did I feel the unpleasant sensation of guilt, which never leaves you once it has seized on you.

During the war, Jude's suicide simplified matters; I could

spend more time down in the cellar with Herman at night. But after the Liberation, when we tried to resume normal life as if nothing had happened, after my sister Anne's rape, my father's return, when I no longer enjoyed teaching at the school, all these wartime incidents came back to my mind, and one question has never ceased to haunt me: Why? Why did Jude commit suicide? Why didn't I see it coming?

The funeral was attended by Jude's family, in black: parents, brothers and sisters, nephews and nieces. It was a big funeral, with large announcements in the local paper. Even the school where I taught paid for a little notice vicariously expressing condolences; but in the corridors of the building itself, in the staff room, not one of my colleagues or pupils came up to say a word to me. Every day brought its own tragedies, yes, there were mitigating circumstances, but was it so difficult to lay a hand on my arm for a few moments as a sign of sympathy, not to say compassion?

For I was not indifferent to that body in my bed, the body of a human being with whom I had lived for eight years of my life. After all, the rest of the world didn't know that we had never touched each other — or could my absence of desire be read in my face? In these days, when you let it all hang out and want to know everything, that might be so, but in 1942, when the French had gotten into the habit of closing their eyes to so much, why should they care

that the marriage of John and Jane Doe had never been con-
summated? I pretended not to notice the lack of feeling
shown by those around me. At the time it did not make me
suffer.

Of course the Church pretended not to know that the death
was suicide. There were so many deaths during the war. My
father-in-law went to the bishop's place, he knew people
there. He stayed in the offices for two hours, and when he
came out Jude had died of hemorrhagic congestion of the
lungs. Mass could be said. I had to sit through the parish
priest's vicious sermon. He managed to pin Jude's death on the
Jews and the lustful atmosphere they had imposed on France
for so many decades. He was an appalling man, and later he
was bumped off, cassock and all. On the day of the Liberation, a Resistance man brought him down outside his own
church with a volley of submachine-gun fire. His body
slumped on one of the stone seats that seem to be holding
up the facade of the building, as if he had simply let himself
drop there in the most natural way in the world after an exhausting celebration of the Eucharist, but with an expression
of stupefaction on his face. You could see he was dead, because
his cassock was riddled with bullet holes. St. Sebastian, one
might have thought, but even more dead. I didn't have the
heart to rejoice that day, I had other things on my mind,
and who relishes an assassination, however well deserved?

)K(K)K(

Apart from the empty place beside me in my bed, Jude's death made little difference to my life. I didn't clear out the wardrobe. Bereaved husbands or wives often get rid of their late spouses' clothes because they cannot bear the sight of anything reminding them of their lost love, but I felt no grief, my mourning was all on the surface, easy to keep going. Jude's clothes could stay hanging in the closet and did not trouble me. I did not take them out. They are still there, you can check if you like, they're terribly dusty because I hate garment bags. The cellar is still as it was, too. I never took the books upstairs again after the war. The reading room is intact, like a souvenir of past times, and of one of the truly happy periods in my life. It is my museum, my Berggasse. I go to rest there when I feel that life is unjust — not every time I feel that, however, or I would spend my days down there.

And was the priest wrong? Could not Jude's suicide be blamed on the Jew I was hiding underground? It made no difference that Herman was Jewish. He was a man. He didn't complain of his confinement in the cellar. He read a great deal. Daylight came in through a tiny window that we had partially blocked up for reasons of security. The small opening looked out on the back of the house, the wall separating us from the Christophes' garden was quite close, and no one used that dark, narrow passage. The mossy ground never saw the sun, and its rays never shone through the little window.

Herman learned whole poems of Heine by heart in this twilight, to exercise his memory. He didn't speak German, but he understood it very well, because of the language I had taken for Berlin dialect when I first heard it in the Gestapo building. Herman spoke Yiddish. I had thought that Jews spoke the language of the country where they lived, like Madame Bloch the draper. However, the Jews of Poland did not speak Polish or even Hebrew; they spoke Yiddish. A language that came from no one knew where, and I understood it. You could have taken it for a slightly adulterated kind of German, now and then using words imported from elsewhere that popped up like jack-in-the-boxes, and amusing, slightly comic turns of phrase. In fact, Herman already knew the poems of Heine by heart, but in Yiddish. He recited them to me.

> *A fikhtnbom shtayt anzam*
> *In tsufn ergetsvi*
> *Im shlefert: in de kalte shnay*
> *Dekt vi a dek im tsi.*

> *Er khulemt fin a palme*
> *Vus shtayt in mizrekh-land*
> *In troyert shtil in anzam*
> *Dort of a felznvant.*

I knew that poem by heart, too, and often recited it. *Ein Fichtenbaum steht einsam*. But it was in a different language, so near, so far. I understood almost all the words, but they made me laugh, they were so curiously distorted. I listened to Herman reciting, I couldn't make his face out very well in the dark cellar. I breathed in the smell of him, the scrap of Marseilles soap I had managed to pilfer mingled with a little of his own scent. His passion for the poetry was in his voice. I would have liked to draw his head toward me and kiss him. I did not move, to all outward appearances I was stone, but inside I was on fire, and I recited the same lines, this time as Heine had written them:

> *Ein Fichtenbaum steht einsam*
> *Im Norden, auf kahler Höh.*
> *Ihn schläfert; mit weisser Decke*
> *Umhüllen ihn Eis und Schnee.*

> *Er träumt von einer Palme*
> *Die, fern im Morgenland,*
> *Einsam und schweigend trauert*
> *Auf brennender Felsenwand.*

For a long time Herman had kept an edition of Heine's poetry in the inside pocket of his coat, the pocket he called his *buzem-keshene*. It was his favorite book. He had to part with it when Maréchal Pétain passed the statute on the Jews; he wanted to avoid showing any sign that he was Jewish. Herman told me that his book was hidden under the roof of a building at 6, rue Marceau, where he was renting an attic room in Madame Pelloux's house at the time. He had left most of his books in Paris, and anyway a friend had burned the few volumes in a coal stove when the Germans invaded. All he had left was his Heine, which might still be at Madame Pelloux's.

Oddly enough, I knew the lady. Well, it wasn't so strange. Ours was a small town, and her daughter was a student of mine in the ninth grade. When Herman was discharged, he had found a room locally; he didn't want to go back to Paris immediately and thought it better to wait and see what happened. Later, his friends in Paris advised him not to return there. We were in the occupied zone, but it was easier to find food in the country, and to hide if need be. The mountains weren't far away.

Madame Pelloux was not a bad woman; her husband had died in the early 1930s from the aftereffects of poison gas at Verdun, and she was bringing up her only daughter, Monique, alone. After the Jewish statute became law she went on renting the room to Herman, which not everyone would have done. Herman had been arrested in her house at dawn one morning, the day I found him in the Gestapo building, but he didn't think Madame Pelloux had denounced him. More likely it was her neighbor Monsieur Besson, a schoolmaster on the arts side and thus a colleague of mine, but at the boys' school. A very well-educated man.

XXXX

I don't remember any reaction at home when we read in the paper about Maréchal Pétain's passing of the Jewish statute. I think we took it as just one of the innumerable decrees issued at the beginning of the Occupation. At least one new law a week affected our daily life. The Jewish law did not; we didn't know any Jews, although at the time I made some discoveries about people I would never have expected to be Jewish — people of good standing like Beaucaire the pharmacist at the rue des Carmes, and Lyon, a judge in the law courts. He was married to one of my mother's childhood friends, but the two women had lost touch with each other. Véronique Lecoeur, whom my mother called la Vonique, I don't know why. Nothing distinguished those Jews from the other people in town, unless it was that we didn't know them so well because we hadn't met their children at catechism class, or in the private schools we attended, or as Scouts and Guides.

I say the Jews, the Jews, but what does that really mean? "The Jews of Poland spoke Yiddish." How do I know? I didn't read that in any book, Herman told me. It was a fact to him because the people in his shabby street in Warsaw spoke Yiddish. But what about other parts of the country, the upper-class parts of Krakow, the resort towns? I read somewhere that the great Polish poet Julian Tuwim was Jewish. So how did he get to be a great Polish poet? By speaking Yiddish with his grandmother?

I wanted to retrieve Herman's volume of Heine. I had to have that wartime treasure. I said nothing to Herman, because I wanted to surprise him. It took me a long time to work out my tactics. Madame Pelloux and Monique must not on any account suspect that I was acquainted with Herman. I knew how to get into the house; Monique was my pupil, and I could easily think up some pretext, but how was I going to make my way into the attic room? The door was sure to be locked, unless the room had been rented again since Herman's arrest.

Monique had never attracted my attention before. She was a mediocre student. She tackled German as a school subject to be learned, and did only what was necessary to get average marks. My colleagues who taught other subjects described her in the same way: a child without any notable enthusiasms, not very lively, a little solitary, rather spoiled by her mother, who had no particular ambition for her daughter. Nothing to arouse my interest.

Purely for my own calculating reasons, I began singling her out in class. I spent more time on her work, and commented on the good ideas in it more than on her clumsy expressions. Now and then, at the end of the lesson, I asked her to come and see me so that I could express my satisfaction with the progress she was making. The sudden attention I was paying her soon affected her attitude. She had been troubled by it at first, seeming not to know how to deal with her emergence from the shadows into which she had retreated. But like any other human being in a similar situation, she was quick to respond to my new show of interest. Her enthusiasm for the German language grew. To everyone's surprise she became one of the hardest-working girls in the class, so that I ended up thinking her less unattractive, in spite of her pimples and the copious dandruff in her pigtails.

My first objective was to get myself invited to tea with her mother, and then I would try to find out how to gain access to the top of the house. Monique made it easy for me. She had liked a poem by Schiller that we studied in class, *Das Mädchen aus der Fremde*. My adult glance had awoken the child to the point where, as I liked to think, she identified with the girl in the poem.

> *Lightly she stepped, all felt her grace,*
> *And knew a swelling of the heart,*
> *Her dignity and bearing chaste*
> *Yet marked her out as set apart.*

She asked me to lend her a book of Schiller's poetry. I said I would, telling myself that I would find a way to use this loan for my own purposes. I lent her an edition in Gothic type, published in Berlin in 1934 in honor of, as the title page said, that patron of German letters Reich Minister of Public Information and Propaganda Dr. Joseph Goebbels. My fellow teachers had given it to me as a wedding present.

A few weeks later, on the pretext of needing this collection of Schiller's poetry back urgently, I phoned on Sunday, taking care to wait until Madame Pelloux and her daughter would be home from Mass. I got myself invited to tea that very afternoon. The house was rather dark, suiting my own idea of a place where a man gassed in the Great War had died: lace doilies, somber curtains. A porcelain shaving bowl hung over the door announced: "Woman Does What the Devil Cannot."

I told Madame Pelloux what a good opinion I had of her daughter, which was not entirely true, but getting Herman's book back mattered more than the truth. Monique blossomed under the rays of my pretended interest, her mother told me how pleased she was to see the change in her daughter, and never mind if she didn't understand anything about German poetry, I would bring Herman his book back like a trophy of war, I would be justified in wearing a Phrygian cap of liberty that day. We all got something out of this conversation, and in the course of it, I found out that Madame Pelloux was living alone in the house with Monique. She had not rented out Herman's room again.

One late February afternoon, when I had given my last lesson of the day to Monique's class, I asked the child to stay behind on the pretext of suggesting more poetry for her to read. During the Romantic period, the towering figures of Goethe and Schiller (I had to omit Heine for fear of compromising myself) had overshadowed certain works notable for their rhythm and sensitivity, by Müller, Bürger, and other writers. We embarked upon a conversation on the subject. To be honest, it was a monologue, for Monique was not the ideal conversational partner in such a discussion. Her knowledge of the language was too limited for her to appreciate its literature. But she was delighted that I had singled her out. She felt she was really someone. And I craftily kept her there talking as I waited for night to fall.

At the end of an hour's conversation in which I forced myself to speak of my passion for certain poems (there was something a little obscene about displaying my emotions to someone whom I hardly knew and whom, at heart, I wanted to know so little), I turned my head to the window and pretended to be astonished to see that it was dark outside. Monique did not understand my vexation, so I explained that I was afraid of going home, because a woman neighbor had been found dead two weeks earlier outside the railings of the public park, with a bullet in her, and I had to pass the same park on my way. No one knew if the murderer was a German soldier who had drunk too much, or a deranged terrorist on a sabotage mission (I didn't know Monique well enough to venture the term *Resistance fighter*). Monique suggested that I could spend the night with them; we only had to cross the road to her house, I had nothing to fear, and the room on the third floor had been empty since Monsieur Herman left.

I was like a hunting dog hearing a partridge move among the leaves, pricking its ears, raising its muzzle. The dog's eye lights up in the true spirit of Diana the huntress, its nose is damp. I made myself keep calm and ask, casually: Monsieur who? Oh, Monique told me, a gentleman who is my mother's lodger, but he hasn't been back to spend the night for quite a long time. She had spoken Herman's name without any emotion, without batting an eyelash; it was odd to hear his name sounding almost neutral in her mouth. Had this adolescent girl never felt anything for the lodger? Seeing him daily, how could she have withstood the charm of the tall Jew with the blue eyes and deep voice, the wide shoulders and generous hands? How could I know what she felt for him? I dared not ask her; I simply taught her German. Officially, I had never met the Herman who disappeared behind Gestapo bars.

I said: Oh, I couldn't. You never know, he might be back this very night. She said: No, that's not possible. I said: Why not? She blushed. I mean, she said, night has fallen, if he had been coming back he'd be here by now. In fact, she knew he would not be back. She knew, without saying so, that people didn't come back from the Gestapo. But where did she think he was? In prison, in a labor camp? Certainly not at the back of my cellar, wearing my underclothes or Jude's, reading Heine in German. I accepted Monique's invitation with pretended reluctance.

As for Madame Pelloux, you'd have thought that Louis XIV had decided to spend the night in her house, or that Nefertiti was coming to dinner. The meal was frugal; this was wartime, and Madame Pelloux was not the kind to resort to the black market, but her manner to me was obsequious in the extreme. She would not let me pay for my meal, but finally accepted the bread coupons I offered her. I usually guarded those coupons jealously, for I had to feed two people on my rations, but now that I was close to achieving my purpose, it was not the moment to skimp on the means to my end.

We talked of this and that during dinner, but not of the war. In those days people who hardly knew each other were careful not to broach the subject. A remark could be exaggerated, distorted, subjected to negative interpretation; a mere cedilla could denounce you. We talked about the countryside around our town, the walks you could take on fine days, all the snow we'd had last winter, the tram, gasogene-powered cars. Madame Pelloux described the winter Sundays of her youth, climbing the mountain up to the Primavère cross, skis over your shoulder, a picnic at the foot of the cross, then skiing down to the valley. Home by tram about four in the afternoon, and a good bowl of onion soup before you went to bed.

Around nine I said good night, on the pretext of having a

great deal of homework to correct for the next day. Madame Pelloux told me there was no heating in my room; I would find it difficult to work in the cold. I replied: I'm used to it these days. She said that I mustn't worry about being cold in the night, because Monique would bring me up a hot-water bottle. She took me up to the third floor, where she opened the only door, the door to Herman's room, an attic with a dormer window that probably looked out on the street. She left me for a few moments to find me a nightshirt, a towel, and a washcloth. She offered to bring me up an herbal tea a little later, and I accepted so as not to offend her, but said that after all I might not correct my homework, so perhaps the tea . . . Paying little attention to what I said, she went out to tell Monique to make the tea and the hot-water bottle at once. She wished me good night, Monique soon came up with her makeshift heating devices, and I was given a chamber pot, for the lavatories were in the courtyard behind the church.

While my carefully planned proximity to my student and her mother was a little embarrassing, I did not fear the immodesty of the chamber pot, not after emptying Herman's every day, not after all the discretion I had to show in looking after a man who was unable to cast aside his physical functions when he entered the cellar. I sometimes thought it would have been more practical to have saved a snake: I could have found it a mouse once every ten days, given it the mouse to eat, it would have spent the next ten days silently digesting the mouse in a corner of the cellar, and at the end of that time I would have found a little dry pellet, an odorless heap of bones and fur that the snake had excreted. I could almost have knitted the snake a mouse-hair blanket. Everything can be recycled.

Monique left, wishing me good night. She would certainly have liked to stay and have a few extra minutes of my company. I pretended to be unaware of her wishes. I closed the door behind her, and now I had all night to find the Heine volume. I began investigating. I took care to make as little noise as possible while I searched the room, for I had said I'd be going to bed early. I began in the most remote parts, for Herman would not have put the book in one of the desk drawers. I very soon did find a book behind a beam in the ceiling. However, it was not in Yiddish, but was written in characters like those around the porch of the synagogue in the rue Thiers: Hebrew. Herman must have mixed them up, and had destroyed the Heine and kept a prayer book by mistake. Or else his memory had let him down, and the Heine was somewhere else (I didn't see how anyone could possibly have burned the greatest of German poets).

I opened the volume in my hands. The Hebrew characters were crooked, baroque, in fact rather beautiful, but I hated being unable to decipher them. Why, when the civilized world had long ago gone over to the Roman alphabet, did the Jews have to keep this outdated writing if not for occult ends? I was still looking at the book, and realized that the page numbers were upside down, the wrong way round, another sign of the disturbing strangeness of the Jews, tying themselves up in knots like that. Yet this explanation did not satisfy me for more than a few seconds after my first surprise. It was the letters that were upside down, of course; I was holding the book the wrong way round. I had opened it with the cover on the left, out of habit, but Hebrew was written from right to left, so it was logical to open a book the other way. The Jews did not write their numbers upside down, they did worse: they opened books the wrong way.

I opened the volume again the right way. It was a disagreeable sensation, like an assault on my education, on the great men who had formed the culture of Europe, France, Germany and other such countries: Montaigne, Luther, Hugo, Leibniz, Spinoza, Goethe, Heine himself. I had read in the press and heard at church that the Talmud was a pernicious book, and I must have some kind of Talmud in my hands, but how could Herman, a man of such delicacy of mind, turn to reading such things?

Where was I? In a room which was not mine, in the house of one of my pupils, holding a Hebrew Talmud belonging to a Jew I loved. I clutched the book to my chest like a body I wanted to hold close. I was embracing a void rather than flesh, but it was a small part of Herman all the same. My fingertips were frozen. I was beginning to shiver. I must get into bed to make the most of the warmth still in the hot-water bottle. I drank the tisane, a small, hot comfort in my distress, I put on the nightshirt — whose was it? — and slipped into the warm bed. I picked up that strange book again, opening it at the beginning, and facing the title page I found some wording in roman characters:

HEINRICH HEINE
GEDICHTE
VERLAG NEULAND (S. J. IMBER), WIEN, 1920

It was Herman's Heine. So Yiddish was written like Hebrew, from right to left and in Hebrew characters. But then how could it be like German? I spent some time examining the pages, which told me little. I hated not being able to start reading; these Jews and their secret writing annoyed me. Piqued, I finally put out the light, but I had difficulty getting to sleep. Those abstruse characters worried me. In spite of everything, I pleasured myself before going to sleep. Hadn't I earned that fleeting release?

I cannot have looked very refreshed the next day when I said good-bye to Madame Pelloux and Monique after breakfast. I had no lessons that morning, so I went home. My mother was polishing the kitchen floor and said she had been anxious when I didn't come home last night; it wasn't like me to stay out without warning. I didn't tell her where I had spent the night, and she did not press me to say; I was an adult. Perhaps she thought I was seeing someone. I had every right to, for my mourning was officially over, and my sister Anne's conduct gave me a certain latitude. It isn't what you imagine, I thought. I didn't spend the night in the arms of someone I love, I was simply trying to understand part of his mystery.

Herman must have wondered why I hadn't been down to see him the previous night, but he would have to wait for an explanation; I couldn't go down to the cellar that morning because my mother was in the kitchen. My sister must have been asleep, but she would soon wake up. Herman would wait patiently until evening before I came to empty his chamber pot, and as for food, I had taken him down plenty the evening before, enough to see him through the day. I went back to my room, locked the door, put the Heine on my desk, opened the *Larousse Encyclopedia* at the page showing the Hebrew alphabet, and began deciphering it. I opened the book at random; it was page forty-six. I kept my right forefinger on the first character. With my left forefinger, I looked for its counterpart in the table in *Larousse*. *Shin*, a *sh* sound. Then *ayin, e; non, n; ayin, e* again. After a few minutes I had the first word:

שענע

Shene. Then the second: *vig.* It wasn't long before I had the whole first line: *shene vig fun meyne leyden.* Very soon I had the whole of the first verse, which I transcribed on a sheet of paper so that I could try reading it all through:

shene vig fun meyne leyden
shene kvr fun meyn ruh
shene shtodt, ikh muz zikh sheyden —
zey gesund! vinsh ikh dir tsu.

I had learned this poem in my last year at school; I remembered having to know it by heart for my baccalaureat exam. A song of love and nostalgia, a man leaving his birthplace and the girl he loves. The German words came back to me, and I whispered them:

Schöne Wiege meiner Leiden,
Schönes Grabmal meiner Ruh,
Schöne Stadt, wir müssen scheiden
Lebe wohl! Ruf' ich dir zu.

The music that Robert Schumann had composed for this *Lied* was going through my head, it's the music we were listening to just now, *Schöne Wiege meiner Leiden*. As I recalled the melody, I was remembering a recital I had attended with Hans-Joachim near Heidelberg in 1930. The singer, who had a fine baritone voice and graying hair, rested his hand on the piano and closed his eyes after each *Lied* as if to help him compose his mind before tackling the next song. He took himself so seriously that it was almost comic, but we were in Germany, where music is indeed a serious matter, too serious, no doubt, and we couldn't laugh. The pianist was a girl, very young, perhaps twenty, and the audience, apart from Hans-Joachim and me, consisted of German aristocrats.

The recital was given in the music room of a castle in the middle of a forest. I don't remember now just how we came to be there. Was one of our teachers related to the baroness bedecked in emu feathers who received us? Was the pianist a girlfriend of Hans-Joachim's? That detail has been lost along the way in my memory. I do remember arriving at night. We had come on foot, over an hour's walk. Luxury cars were waiting outside the castle, each with its chauffeur. It was a very intimidating scene. We felt out of place, we were the poor relations, that's how I remember that evening. But most of all I remember Hans-Joachim's thigh brushing against mine, and the mannerisms of the singer.

The music had remained very clear in my mind, because my German friend had given me a record, which I played over and over again on my parents' gramophone until it was worn out and inaudible. *Schöne Wiege meiner Leiden.* Recently I bought it again, the very same performance, but this time on a CD, the one I've just played you. What they call a remastered version, or maybe you could call it repasteurized. Some technician has spent hours at a computer taking out all the crackling; the place where I bought the disc had a certificate of its skill in the restoration of audio recordings, and the salesman told me that the crackling sounds are called clicks and clacks, or maybe it's cliques and claques, I haven't found them in any dictionary. When you repasteurize a recording you take away the clicks and clacks with just the tap of a finger on the mouse, and presto! or rather click! the disc doesn't crackle any more, all you have left is the music.

In my youth records crackled. Couldn't we have a crackling version, Monsieur Specialist? It was a shocking suggestion. But I wanted the fairest cradle of my sorrows, something authentic, the fairest tombstone of my peace, I wanted the *Lieder* just as they used to be with all their clicks and clacks, the music room in Baden-Württemberg and the condescending barons who came with it. And Hans-Joachim beside me, his thigh against mine. The poet was saying farewell to his native city. *City fair, we part tomorrow.* I had never even wished Hans-Joachim good luck. Our correspondence foundered in the whirlpools of the 1930s, and I don't know what became of him. Another enigma.

שענע וויג פון מיינע ליידען
שענער קבר פון מיין רוה
שענע שטאָדט, איך מוז זיך שיידען
זיי געזונד ! ווינש איך דיר צו.

I was reading Heine in Yiddish. I didn't dare do it out loud. It was too new to me, how could I know if my pronunciation was right? Where foreign languages are concerned I have always been very demanding, of others and of myself, it's an occupational hazard. I repeated the verse several times until I knew it by heart. I was preparing myself for Herman. I wanted to bring him that poem like an offering.

86

You often saw photographs of children reciting eulogies to
Maréchal Pétain in newspapers of the time. Suddenly I was
ten years old again, preparing for my captive hero. I had
spent all morning deciphering that verse, but I stumbled
over the words. I had German rhythms in my head, the
music of Heine's words and Schumann's melody, and the
Yiddish lines did not seem to respect them.

That afternoon at school, Monique tried to meet my eye,
keeping the complicity between us going. I smiled at her at
the beginning of the lesson, and spent the rest of it avoiding
her. The Pelloux family were part of my past, I no longer
needed them. All the same, I would have to go on pretending to take an interest in Monique so as not to suffer the ef-
fects of her disappointment. Envy and jealousy filled the
prison cells of this war, and few felt any scruples about it.

I dined at the family table alone with my mother. Anne was
out. She had to welcome Danielle Darrieux, returning radiant from her trip to Berlin, unless it was some other event in
aid of the war effort that evening. I talked about this and
that with Mother. She asked me questions about school; I
replied. I asked her if there was any news of Papa. She hadn't
had another letter, but the last was dated barely five days ago.
My father seemed to be all right. He was getting enough to
eat, and that was what mattered. He wouldn't be back very
soon, he was too healthy: only the sick were repatriated.

We had given up drinking coffee after dinner because of

the expense. My mother was not the sort of woman who drank herb tea, so we sold the lime-tree blossoms from our garden. I told my mother I would wash the dishes, and she went upstairs to bed.

My father had a mistress in Germany. After several weeks in the Stalag, he was sent to a farmer to help him work the land. As the farmer lived some way from the camp, my father slept at the farm and had to report regularly to the authorities in charge of the prisoners. At the end of 1943 the German farmer was drafted. His sons were already at the front, and had been there a long time. My father was left alone to run the farm with the farmer's wife, one thing led to another and he ended up in her bed. Of course my father didn't tell us this story when he came home. He told us life there had not been easy, he had missed his house and his mountains, too. The Germans to whose house he'd been sent were rustics. They ate straight off the table. The plates were hollows worked into the wood, and you filled them with food. No dishes to wash, just a wipe with a cloth to clean them out for the next meal, so much for hygiene. But that was nothing to the trials others had endured.

So far the story was like a little cloth book I had as a child. A book for tiny paws, my parents called it. There was a pig on one page, a cow on another, a sheep, a chicken yard with hens, a rooster and some baby chicks, a blonde farmer's wife setting briskly off for the fields, basket over her arm, a little boy smiling as he collected eggs. The book did not invite its young readers into the farmer's bed to see what my father did there with the farmer's wife. I learned the end of the story much later, after my mother's death. I was looking for a secondhand car, and dealing with an old insurance agent who had only one arm. People used to frighten their children by telling them he had lost his arm sticking it out of the door of his car. I bought a 204 coupe from him, I didn't have children, it was ideal.

On the day of the sale he offered me a glass of Chambolle-Musigny; this was before the invention of the Breathalyzer. The insurance agent said he had known my father well. They had been in the same unit, they were in the Stalag together, and he told me the whole story. I didn't let him think I knew it already; he'd have been disappointed, and I still wanted him to give me a discount on the car insurance. But I did put up a show of indifference, suggesting that we each have to paddle our own canoe. In fact, the insurance agent had lost his arm in 1940.

I washed the two plates as I waited for Mother to fall asleep. I wiped them drier than ever, there was not the faintest trace of moisture left on the surface, it was impeccable, a really professional job. I quietly climbed the stairs to the half-landing, because I couldn't see Mother's room from the ground floor. The crack under the door told me that her light was out. I went downstairs again. I unlocked the cellar door and locked it again behind me with my duplicate key. It was a dark night, but I knew the way by heart: fifteen wooden steps, the last one higher than the others. I went into the wine cellar, feeling for the necks of the bottles with my left hand, and reached the back wall where the crates were piled up. I unblocked the hole, mustn't give way to impatience, the crates might crash to the floor, I only hoped my mother wouldn't take it into her head to burn them as firewood one day. I delicately put the paving stones on the floor, must remember where the crates were and not put a stone on top of them.

I unblocked the hole, climbed through, too bad about my pale clothing, you couldn't see anything in the dim light. Herman was standing there waiting for me. A candle was burning behind him; he was visible in silhouette.

"Where were you?"

"My mother went up to bed late."

"I was waiting for you."

"I couldn't come last night. I had to get a book back from a pupil."

I had meant to keep the poem for later, choose the right moment, but the reproach in Herman's voice precipitated matters and the poem escaped my lips:

> *shene vig fun meyne leyden*
> *shene kvr fun meyn ruh*
> *shene shtodt, ikh muz zikh sheyden —*
> *zey gesund! vinsh ikh dir tsu.*

He said nothing. Then he burst out laughing, with wounding irony.

"Who taught you the poem? Where does that pronunciation come from?"

"Isn't it right?"

"That depends. Not in Warsaw. Maybe in Wilno, as recited by the head of the Protestant faculty of theology!"

> *shayne vig fin mane laden*
> *shayner kayver fin ma ri*
> *shayne shtuet, kh'miz zakh shaden —*
> *za gezint! vinsh ikh diye tsi.*

All this Jew down in his hole had noticed was my funny pronunciation. The enormous gift I was giving him left him cold. I took the Yiddish book out of my bag and dumped it on the table with an angry gesture. It was dark; Herman didn't recognize the book at first glance.

"Here, this is for you, it was behind a beam."

Herman picked up the book. He moved away to take it over to the candle, almost turning his back to me. He opened the book, caressed a page. No more laughter or reproaches. I think he was moved. He said nothing. His hands were trembling slightly. He turned and looked at me. He wasn't crying. I wanted him to cry. He embraced me fervently. At that moment, I think he loved me.

We made love on the beaten earth floor to stifle any sounds. I took his penis in my mouth, and he came in me. It was so good to feel him, that Jew inside me. That man, just for me. His hands grasped my buttocks, his tongue licked my ears. He was just rough enough to dominate me, but attentive to what I wanted, too. I had never felt such orgasms, my loins burned with the pleasure that Jude had never given me, my skin was tingling all over, I felt joy I had never known before.

I had been waiting for this man so long. No one else could have occupied the place that awaited him, not my father, nor any of my teachers, not Hans-Joachim, who had never touched me sensuously, still less my headmaster at school or the priest who taught catechism classes. Herman was here, I had improvised his abduction — only my desire for him had dictated my heroic conduct, the escape from the Gestapo, the hiding place in the cellar, the translation of Heine. I had succeeded in getting him to come to me, although there was no reason to think in advance that anything in me could arouse such savage desires. His way of making love to me left it in no doubt: he was lord and master of my body, he had taken it with the appetite of a cannibal, no part of it was spared, not my thighs, my pubis, my nipples. I let him seize upon me because I had to. I was a living human being. At last.

5

For a while literature retreated into the background of our relationship. Heine, Mann, Rilke and the others waited patiently on their shelves. We had something better to do: make love. As soon as I arrived in the cellar by night Herman flung me down on the floor; he had been bottling up his desire all day. He undressed me, penetrated me, I was like a chicken on the spit offered up to the flames, and I liked it. I wanted those violent orgasms. To make any noise could have been our undoing; suppressing my cries was torment. I would have liked to lose control entirely, because it was so good and it would have been better to cry it out loud.

I thought of my sister spread like a sow under Volker's

body. Or no, I imagined her on her belly, really like an animal, breasts crushed to the mattress, Volker lying on top of her and rummaging roughly about in her. How could an SS man be other than rough? My sister made the walls of the house shake with her orgasms, yet I had to force my own body to keep silent; I stuffed the patchwork blanket we had made into my mouth, and my groans were muted into murmurs. My muffled cries became sweaty sobs. My body was drenched after we had made love. Herman was sweating, too, he couldn't control himself. Which coupling was more monstrous, Anne and Volker's, or mine with Herman?

"Our love is against Nazi law."

"I know."

He had said *love*.

"Aren't you afraid?"

"My body is sodden with fear."

"You're risking death."

"So are you."

"But I was risking death already without you."

"Well, now we can face it together."

At any other time our love would have weighed on me like a sin. I was coupling with this Jew, while Jude had bled to death from opened veins, but I felt pride in it. Jude was close, just on the other side of the partition, or the memory of Jude in any case. But our life together, no passion, no sweat, no penetration, was light years away from the conflagration in this cellar.

XOXOX

Were all Jews such extraordinary lovers as Herman? Was their talent for sex the reason why people hunted them down to exterminate them? Or was Herman just a lover like any other, but one who had nothing left but lovemaking in this cellar and some lines of Heine to perfect? The secrecy heightened our sensations. Having to reach a climax in silence was frustrating, but didn't the ceremony that brought me to those heights of pleasure make up for the necessity of keeping quiet? Climbing in as if through a mouse hole, going down underground, moving the paving stones and crates, lying down on that makeshift mattress, and, above all, disappearing into a little core of the terrestrial globe where the earth seized us, existing no longer, being dead to all others but ten thousand times alive to ourselves, forgetting everything, my students, homework, Chinese porcelain, Bruges lace, Heine, Hölderlin, lying on the earth, why do I say earth? My soil, the soil of France, but down in a cellar. Feeling its coolness on my belly, the beaten earth under the palms of my hands, stricken, humiliated, it soiled and humiliated me. I tasted it with the tip of my tongue, I licked it, I licked it again, it was bitter, it was good.

The cellar was a secret den where nothing could happen to us, for the world did not know about our union. No one was looking for Herman. The clerk who kept the Gestapo records hadn't written his name in the register yet when I abducted him. My sister protected us, thanks to Volker. I'd been well advised not to kill him, even if my stomach always turned at the sight of him. You often don't know what a service you may be doing yourself by leaving certain things undone.

The war went on. The Allies landed in North Africa, my sister Anne, unmoved, continued her relations with Volker, the Germans occupied the free zone, the Resistance resisted, fixers sold butter, eggs and cheese at prohibitive prices which my salary as an employee of the French state put beyond me. I had to make do with my official rations, which I shared. Herman was moldering away down in the cellar. As far as I could see in the dim light, his skin was bleached. If the war went on much longer, mushrooms would be growing on him, and the same fate awaited my books.

Herman took to doing exercises for hours on end, to pass the time, to keep from dying of cold, and so that he could go on seducing me, for I wanted his body and he knew it. His skin was blanched like an endive, but it stretched taut over his muscles in spite of the small amount of protein I brought back from the hunt for ration coupons. I loved him. If I hadn't, I don't think I could have looked after him. It was so much work, such a constant anxiety, pretending that everything was normal but always keeping an eye in the back of my head to make sure that Volker or Anne didn't see me going down to the cellar, that nothing in my bearing could give away his presence.

At school the teachers saw me in the same light as ever, an easygoing colleague, vaguely in mourning still, with two known passions: the German language, and the literature written in it. If some of them kept their distance it must have been because my specialty was less acceptable outside school at this time than Greek or mathematics, not because of the love that I had to keep secret.

If I had not enjoyed making love with Herman so much, I feel sure I would have gotten rid of him in the end. I would have forgotten to close the cellar door one day, I would have brought the volume of Heine in Yiddish upstairs and forgotten to take it off the breakfast table when Volker went into the kitchen, zipping up his fly; I would have left my Jew's full chamber pot on the shelf in the lavatory. Volker would have recognized its contents as Jewish shit, he'd have called his little friends in to search the house, and they'd have found Herman and taken him away. Or I would have cried out loud one night when he was making love to me, just once to make up for all the times I had had to keep quiet, and the whole neighborhood would have come running, thinking someone was cutting a pig's throat in the cellar. But it would have been only one more Jew to be taken away and driven off in a truck, assuming he had nothing worth taking first, no silverware, no money hidden in the mattress, no rolls of cloth to make dresses for the caretaker's daughters, not even gold teeth — too young for that — only an indecipherable old book published in Vienna in 1920.

I kept going for selfish reasons. I couldn't do without him. It was true love.

And what about him? Did he love me? Yes, that evening when I brought him back his book. Did he realize, afterwards, that he could survive only by keeping my love alight? My fingers explored every part of his body during our nights together. I could have recognized him among a thousand others if I had been blindfolded and told to find him by touch alone — a little blind tasting — but he hadn't told me much about his life. Born in Warsaw just after the war (the first war, that is). Came to France to enroll at the university but had no time to study, he wanted to make the most of Paris, the Grands Boulevards, the cinema, and he had to live and eat, too, that is to say, he had to survive. It was the Grands Boulevards in the evening but the sewing machine all day long. He was paid for piecework. The boss was some kind of cousin. His parents were still in Poland.

"Are you married?"

No reply. There'd been the war, declared on September 1, 1939, anxiety about his parents. He joined up, was sent to the provinces, other foreigners were sent to the front but he wasn't, no idea why not, just chance. Then made general assistant for the intelligence services — surprising in a big lad like him, perhaps because his right lung was a little weak — courier work, taking the mail around, bringing documents for translation. Bringing them where? To you! I'd never know any more, the rest was lovemaking on a beaten earth floor, lovemaking in silence, without a word. And literature, Schiller, Heine.

There was that book, of course, hardly a book really, more of a pamphlet, fifty-four pages to be read from right to left. Facing the title page I had already seen the information in Roman type: copyright by Verlag Neuland (S. J. Imber), Wien. On the same page, a little above that, a phrase in Yiddish saying something else:

SH. Y. IMBERS BIBLIOTEK
(IBERZETSUNGEN FUN DER VELTLITERATUR)

Who was this S. J. Imber who kept so busy translating "world literature" into Yiddish? I longed to know, but would I find his name in a reference book? I tried my *Larousse Encyclopedia* but found nothing; the encyclopedia wasn't interested in minor intellectuals from Central Europe. I tried the university library, on the pretext of looking for a rare edition of *Elective Affinities*. The big German encyclopedias said nothing about Imber the Viennese publisher either. In the library catalogue I found the details of a *Jüdisches Lexicon* in five volumes, published in Berlin from 1927 to 1930. Perhaps I might find some trace of the Viennese with his raspberry-flavored name there, but it wasn't at all likely that if I gave the librarian its reference number I would be able to look at it. If it hadn't been withdrawn from the library stocks, I would be told it had gone missing. I didn't even try. The librarian knew me well, and I didn't want to make myself conspicuous.

I knew nothing else about this Imber. He occupied my mind for only a few days; I was absorbed in our fevered nights in the cellar and my deciphering of Heine in Yiddish. I came to read it more easily, and I learned the forty-two *Lieder* in the book. I knew them in German already, so I was able to recite them bilingually, no doubt the only person in the world who could. After the war, I'd be able to hire myself out to a circus, I'd be more unusual than the bearded woman, less horrifying than the man without limbs.

I did find out a little more about S. J. Imber. Other publications were advertised at the end of the book. In the same Sh. Y. Imbers bibliotek series, he had published *Der sotsyalizm un dem mentshns neshome* by Oscar Wilde (I had some trouble identifying "Oskar Ouayld" as the famous British writer, author of *The Soul of Man under Socialism*), *Di kunst fun dertselen* by Jakob Wassermann, and two works of his own as well: *Viktoria*, subtitled "On the novellas of Knut Hamsun," and *Vald oys, vald ayn,* which was poetry. He announced other forthcoming texts, new editions of his own works (where had they previously been published?), many translations and a study of *The Poetic Legacy of Oscar Wilde*.

Mr. Raspberry (I found out later that *Imber* meant "ginger" in Yiddish, like German *Ingwer*, not *Himbeer*, "raspberry") showed a deep interest in Oscar Wilde. I was surprised to find a Jewish poet feeling an affinity with a writer who had landed in a Victorian jail for indecent behavior. I had never read Wilde's works, since they were banned from the religious institutions where I had been educated. I promised myself that I would make up for it later, after the war, perhaps, when German literature would loosen its hold on me, but I never did: I am still innocent of the writings of Oscar Wilde.

The memory of this man Imber came back to me much later. Over twenty years after the war, I was in the flea market and found a curious four-volume dictionary of Yiddish writers published in Wilno in the 1920s. I had not read any Yiddish since the war, the dictionary cost almost nothing, who would be interested in it? I bought it. There were the imprints of two rubber stamps on the endpapers. One said: "M. Cymbalista — Ladies' Ready-to-Wear Clothing," and the other: "Beaune-la-Rolande Internment Camp."

Looking through it slowly to decipher the names of the writers, making an effort to remember those squared-off characters, I spotted the entry for Imber. In fact there were two of them, Shmaryahou and Shmouel-Yankev. The latter had been born in 1889 at Sosov in Galicia (I had trouble finding this wretched place in an atlas), and after the First World War he lived for some time in Vienna, where he had published his translations and several collections of poems. The entry listed all the publications mentioned in the book I had held in my hands over twenty years earlier. His study of Oscar Wilde had never been published. I learned that one of his most notable collections was *Royzenbleter,* erotic poems published in Wilno in 1914. I would have liked to read those *Rose Leaves,* but I had no way of getting hold of them. You didn't find books in Yiddish in my part of the world. I might perhaps have been able to lay hands on the collection in Paris, New York or Tel Aviv, but I did not visit those cities, and what would I gain by reading the poems? The war was over. Only rats now inhabited the cellar.

6

MATTERS BECAME MORE COMPLICATED when the British took it into their heads to bomb the town. The targets of the air raids were a factory in the suburbs which made caterpillar tracks for tanks and the barracks in the town center, a place that lay between our house and the school and was stuffed with the Boche. When they bombed the factory, they hit a bull's-eye first time off. It was night, we heard the throbbing of the aircraft engines first, a dull and continuous sound, and very soon the municipal sirens began howling. The fire station was three houses away, and the sound of the siren deafened the whole quarter.

Bombs began dropping. I didn't know they were bombs

until later, they were far away, explosions muted by distance. The sirens frightened us most. My mother ran into my room, saying: Quick, down to the cellar, hurry. I went downstairs ahead of my sister. I pretended to be very scared, and talked to my mother in a very loud voice so that Herman would realize I had company. We settled down in the wine cellar on the earth floor. I was praying to heaven that Herman would not move; my mother and sister mustn't know about his presence. I kept talking all the time to make a noise and cover up any movements he might make. But he made none; he was lying low at the bottom of his hole, I imagined him on his makeshift mattress, silent and motionless like a recumbent effigy in a basilica.

The air raid did not last long, but there was more bombing over the next few days. The barracks was a few hundred meters from our house, so the bombs aimed at it dropped very close to us. Down in the cellar the bottles jingled in their metal racks, making a sound just like the chandelier during Anne and Volker's amorous frolics. Again this time, Anne was underground with us. A few crates separated her from my lover, while hers was risking his life in the barracks under attack from the British bombardment. During the air raids I had Herman on my mind, so close that I felt his breath. The next day he told me he had been thinking of me, too, and confessed that he had spent one raid with his hand inside his trousers: if he was going to die of suffocation in a cellar he wanted to do it in my company.

One night the earth shook even more, and part of the cellar ceiling fell in over the racks of bottles. Wine flowed, clouds of dust invaded the cellar, we were choking and paddling around in a sludge of Chassagne-Montrachet Premier Cru; my great fear was that Herman would start coughing and give himself away. I said: Let's go up, don't let's stay here like rats. The all-clear had sounded, but I still had to get my mother and sister out of the cellar, leaving Herman to fend for himself and breathe as best he could.

Another time the sirens went off in the middle of the day. I was correcting homework and found Anne in the cellar with Volker. I hadn't heard him arrive and almost died of fright at the thought of Volker and Herman in the same place. A few minutes later I had made up my mind. If Volker discovered Herman, I would kill him — Volker, I mean. I had no choice. I dreamed of it all through the air raid, and if my sister had not been there I'd have done it, I'd have broken a bottle over his head, liquidated him with some Pinard, smashed his jaw with a Chassagne. I'd have brought a Santenay down on the nape of his neck and then finished him off with the corkscrew, just tap this barrel for me, will you? Blood would have flowed thick and fast, wine, too, a true fountain of youth.

My sister was there and I did nothing. Volker went back to the barracks after the raid. He hadn't had his usual ration of fun, nor had Anne.

XOXOX

The air raids went on for two weeks. People were killed, injured, went missing. The Resistance had the good idea of blowing up the barracks themselves; I don't know whether the operation had been planned long ago or if the decision was made to put an end to the air raids. I was at school one morning, teaching the sixth grade how to conjugate the verb *to have*, when the windows of the building blew out. We were terrified, always terrified, we never stopped being terrified all through that war. Half of my students were in tears, some had been hit in the face by splinters of glass and were bleeding, others had fainted.

The town was in shock. The headmaster told us to go home at once, he didn't know what had happened but he feared German reprisals, hostages picked from the schoolgirls or the teaching staff. The school was closed for several days. Then the boys' grammar school was billeted on us, since its own buildings had been requisitioned to accommodate the soldiers. We had to share classrooms, boys in the morning, girls in the afternoon. Some of the schoolboys had been shot, some of their teachers, too, and the headmaster of the boys' school had disappeared into the Hôtel des Barres. As an example. Why were women never taken as hostages? Because they didn't have the vote yet? My headmaster was promoted: he now ruled all the high school students in town, boys and girls alike.

I quickly left the classroom and ran home. I found my

mother and sister there, and our windows smashed in. By now we knew it was the barracks that had been blown up, no doubt by the Resistance. Volker, who was there, was just off to rejoin his command. He had survived again, the horrible man always did. What luck, he was always lucky, the explosion should have cut him down in his prime, should have routed that fleshy body, sent him running for his life. I hoped he'd be shot for desertion, but that was a waste of time: no use counting on the Germans to get rid of him for us. If I wanted to see him dead, I'd have to do the deed myself.

I had to stay with Anne and my mother. I wanted to do only one thing, go down to the cellar to make sure that Herman was all right and to reassure him about myself. I had to wait for evening. I was obliged to occupy myself all day, find something to do, homework to correct, a lesson to prepare. Anne was waiting for news of her Boche. Did she really love him? I had thought he was a toy for a woman widowed early, a rattle for a girl not as young as she used to be, but she seemed really anxious to know where he was. I had to pretend I hadn't a care in the world: I'm calm because I'm not waiting for any living soul, I'm unperturbed, almost desensitized, I don't have anyone in my life, not the shadow of a love, particularly not in the cellar beneath your feet, Mother, under the soles of your shoes, sister, oh, is he dead now, the man I love, I need his body as you need Volker's but I love his soul, too, even if they go on at us all day long in the papers, over the radio from the Palais Berlitz, telling us the Frères Lissac, opticians, are not to be confused with the Frères Isaac, Jews and dogs are not allowed in the Vuitton store, and a Jewish soul cannot be lovable. So tell me, how about an SS man's soul?

If he dies I die. It's not the same as with Jude. I can go on living after that death because Jude was not one of my vital organs. Herman is me. His eyes his mouth his accent his prick his Heine with all its proto-germanic mumbo jumbo, a twittering sound like speaking German while munching kosher meat, his good humor even kept there in the dim light all day long, while I'm melancholy in broad daylight, in the sun, at the music hall. Herman cheers me, lightens my sadness, burns me, pricks me with his sewing machine, stitching a buttonhole from top to toe, *bbbbbbrrrrrr*, my skin slips past at a lively pace under the presser foot, I am marked with a sore going right through my body, the sore is infected, I love it, its burning does me good, it lights me up.

By the end of the afternoon I couldn't stay at home anymore, half dead of anxiety. I got on my bicycle and rode through town, out into the suburbs, into the country to pass the time, exhausting myself while I waited.

He nearly went mad that day, pacing about like a caged lion. His good humor was gone; his patience had its limits, and now I was discovering them. I loved him in his fury. He was burning to know what had happened. I told him: the barracks were done for, but Volker is alive. He said: Well, I'm going to do you now, it's your turn, and pointed to the mattress. His fear and the waiting had sharpened his appetite. I was his fresh meat, a haunch of antelope put out to pasture. The lion would feast on my body as it lay distended with pleasure.

After several weeks literature reclaimed its right to the cellar. Not that we stopped making love, but we went back to talking before and after. We were emerging from several weeks of mute passion. What were we, when we were together?

I had come upon Else Lasker-Schüler's *Mein blaues Klavier.*

> *Ich habe zu Hause ein blaues Klavier*
> *Und kenne doch keine Note.*
> *Es steht im Dunkel der Kellertür*
> *Seitdem die Welt verrohte.*
>
> *Es spielen Sternenhände vier*
> *— die Mondfrau sang im Boote —*
> *Nun tanzen die Ratten im Geklirr.*
>
> *Zerbrochen ist die Klaviatür . . .*
> *Ich beweine die blaue Tote.*
> *Ach liebe Engel öffnet mir*
> *— ich ass vom bitteren Brote —*
> *mir lebend schon die Himmelstür —*
> *auch wider dem Verbote.*

"*Mein blaues Klavier.*"

"Don't call me that."

"*Man bloe pyane.*"

"I'm not your blue piano."

"In your way you are. You turn up in the evening when I've been moping around all day. You never say anything about your life up there in the daylight."

"It's so unimportant."

"Don't you like your job?"

"Yes, a lot. But what counts is coming here, crawling to you, seeing you, knowing we're safe together, hearing what you've read, Werfel, Kafka, today Else Lasker-Schüler. But I'm not your blue piano. That poem's too sad."

"I read Kafka less and less. It's not a good idea in a cellar; you risk going mad. Lasker-Schüler's mad already, that's different. Do you understand, *mein blaues Klavier?*"

Herman read, he devoured my books by day and me by night. The meaning of some German words eluded him, and he would ask me about them in the evening. I could have lent him a dictionary, but I liked to know he needed me. *Tugend, Schicksal, Friedhof, Mond.* How did you say those words in Yiddish? I asked. *Tsidkes, goyrl, baysoylem, le-vune.* Words stolen from Hebrew. Why had the Jews gone looking for these weird terms when there were words available in German?

"You said why: Because they're Jews."

"So virtue is a Jewish quality? So the moon's Jewish?"

"In a way, maybe."

"You mean its hidden face."

"No, just in the way Jews have of looking at it."

The Jews had taken hold of German, twisted and bent it and then bent it again to make it suit their view of the world. I didn't understand that view, because Herman could not really describe it. He was an unassuming tailor from Warsaw who had hardly had any education. What he knew he had taught himself. He had found literature for himself, thanks to books borrowed from workers' libraries where other unassuming little tailors went in the evening after work to read the newspaper, or to borrow Jules Verne and Knut Hamsun translated into Yiddish. Or Heine. He knew nothing about religion.

I'd never gotten past that chapter of the Bible which tells us how the Jews killed Christ; the catechists always made much of that passage for the benefit of children of my generation, and now here I was in a cellar with one of the murderers' descendants, although he didn't care a whit for either Christ or Moses (he said Moses never existed, and it was all nonsense made up by the rabbis). He swore by literature alone.

"God, God, can't you talk about anything else? I wish you'd stop asking questions about the God of the Jews. I grew up in a Jewish kingdom, you had to walk miles in Warsaw before you saw anyone Polish. Jews everywhere, on the trams, on café terraces, in public parks, in the workshops.

Only Jewish children in the courtyards of apartment buildings. In twenty years' living in Warsaw I didn't hear anything much about God. People didn't spend their time thinking about him, or looking at him hanging on his cross ten feet up above the ground like you do. Some people kept the commandments, some didn't."

"But the people who kept the commandments must have believed in God!"

"Oh, I don't know. My grandfather had a beard almost down to the ground, but he never talked to me about God. He asked if I'd done everything I ought to do. That was what mattered to him, doing what you ought to do. Eating kosher food, keeping the Sabbath, having children — lots of children, because God commands that we must be fruitful and multiply — studying the Torah, learning its prayers."

"So surely the prayers talk about God?"

"Maybe. I don't know Hebrew. I speak Yiddish. *Got,* yes, that's fine, but the *Adonay* of the prayers always seemed a long way off."

"Then what are all those prayers for?"

"For telling you what time it is, morning, noon, and evening. You people have churches with belltowers chiming out the time every quarter of an hour. We were too poor to own watches, and there wasn't any church in my quarter because only Jews lived there. So we prayed. When I had a little money and I could afford to buy a watch, I stopped praying. I remember the day when I confessed to my father that I'd gone into a Polish inn to eat. He hit me. Hit me harder than he ever had in my life. As he saw it, I wasn't a Jew anymore."

"And don't you pray anymore either?"

"I stopped when I was sixteen. I wanted to *be* someone, something else, not a Jew, a normal inhabitant of the world. I didn't want people looking down on me. Still, it all caught up with me at the other end of Europe, in Madame Pelloux's house. Just as I was just getting up in the morning. *Papiere bitte,* your papers, please. I went back to praying in this cellar. I'm a Jew again, aren't I? I mustn't lose track of the passing days. So I just say a prayer, a little *Shma-Yisroel* morning and in the evening. I skip the one at noon."

And what was I? Less than a *Shma-Yisroel?* I went down to be with him every night, but my presence didn't keep him from losing track of the passing days, he needed the prayers for that. I dared not ask him what I was to him just then. I couldn't stop thinking that the Jew who made violent love to me also said his prayers in Hebrew morning and night, an odd occupation in an odd sort of literary salon, just one more of the little follies of this war. I hoped to have him for my own all day, in broad daylight, not just down in the cellar by night. He'd be able to tell the time from the clock then, he could check the passing of the days on a post office calendar like everyone else, without getting all pious and swaying back and forth; he could safely read Kafka. He would make love to me morning, noon, and night. I would be his *Shma-Yisroel,* as he said. But that idea was another folly.

I didn't wait until I could take him up to the ground floor to give him a post office calendar. My mother had two that year, and I took one of them for Herman, hoping he might stop praying. It said, in large letters: "Happy 1943." Herman thanked me when I brought it down to him; it wasn't such a good present as the Yiddish version of Heine. We did make love that day, but it had nothing to do with the calendar. The year passed. My birthday is on December 28. I was planning to take him the 1944 calendar I'd dug up I don't know where. There was another year of war ahead, as ever when the Prussians don't have their way, my grandmother would have said. Herman had marked off all the days on the old calendar. I had told him the date of my birthday, and he wished me a happy birthday that day and read me a poem by Heine, first in German, then in Yiddish. I still know it by heart. I'll recite it to you just as he recited it to me.

> *Aus meinen Tränen spriessen*
> *Viel blühende Blumen hervor,*
> *Und meine Seufzer werden*
> *Ein Nachtigallenchor.*

> *Und wenn du mich lieb hast, Kindchen,*
> *Schenk'ich dir die Blumen all',*

Und vor deinem Fenster soll klingen
Das Lied der Nachtigall.

I still remember it even in Yiddish. As I told you, I'm as good as any carnival attraction.

Os mane trern vaksn
Fil bliende blimen afir,
Tsi nakhtigal-gezangen
Vert yeder zifts fin mir.

In vest mikh lib hubn, kind mans,
Shenk ikh dir di blimen al',
In far dan fenster zol klingen
Dus lid fin de nakhtigal.

It's a sad poem. Sung, perhaps, by a mother bending over her child. She offers her tears to the child like armfuls of flowers and hopes her sighs will be heard as the song of a nightingale. It's silly, perhaps, but I understood that poem as a sign of love. Love me, child, I give you these flowers, and may the nightingale's song be heard at your window. Don't you think that was charming — the way my Jew down underground offered me his tears?

After reciting the poem he put his finger on the date December 28 on the post office calendar. It said, "SS Innocents," Holy

Innocents' Day. Calendars are different now. The change must have come at the end of the 1960s. They must have realized the enormity of the thing. The moment Herman put his finger down on December 28 I had a strange feeling. The catechism I had learned rose to my gullet again: King Herod, the hunt for the divine child in his stable where he lay between the ox and the ass as they breathed their warm breath over him, the massacre of the little boys in Bethlehem and all through Judea at the king's command. At the same time I imagined Volker climbing the stairs to the room where my sister lay with her legs spread. He shamelessly clicked the heels of his boots on the staircase; the walnut wood must still bear their metal marks.

Almost thirty years later, at the sight of "Saints Innocents" over December 28 on the calendar, I thought I felt a faint sense of liberation. It was the first thing I looked at — I couldn't help it — after giving the mailman his Christmas box. But very soon, after all, I felt nostalgia for the time when Herman put his finger on the calendar. To console me for being born on such a date, he quickly placed his lips on mine and invaded my mouth. A strange birthday, indeed, that day when I realized that in effect December 28 celebrated the impunity of those who commit atrocities, and then there was the emotion I felt during that interminable kiss, and after that the lovemaking on the mattress at the back of the cellar.

Had I any single reason to complain of my godless Jew? I had never felt any theological enthusiasm. Would I have saved a rabbi with a big beard from the clutches of the Gestapo, would I have hidden him in my cellar? No. I did not like the inevitable smell of old goat given off by even the best kept of beards. All that bushy hair makes a face resemble a pubis at best, a restaurant scullery at worst. I had saved Herman because of his voice humming Chopin nocturnes, and his swelling chest beneath the army tunic. His Jewishness meant little to me. Unless perhaps I saved him in memory of the draper. I don't know, I don't know anymore, it was all so long ago and I was young. Do I have to answer that question?

I read in the papers, and this was long after the war because no one talked of such things directly after it, that a priest in the Aveyron region hid a rabbi for several years in the toolshed of the cemetery behind his church. In exchange for being kept hidden, for food and shelter, the rabbi taught the priest Hebrew. They read the Bible together. The bargain was cut and dried: a verse of the Bible for a piece of bread. When the priest wanted to go on, wanted to read a second verse and listen to the rabbi's interpretation of it, the rabbi could claim another piece of bread. If not, that was that. The whole thing depended on the priest's goodwill. The rabbi was at his mercy.

The rabbi went mad. On the day of the Liberation he addressed the Allies in Aramaic. The priest got a medal for saving a Jew. The Jews thanked him, there were speeches, people even came over from Israel for the occasion. However, he had done it in his own interest, to fill a gap in his knowledge.

But by the time they gave him that medal no one could tell who had been a hero, who had been a traitor, who was cowardly or courageous. It was a time when people thought they saw in black and white, but they didn't, they only saw gray; that was a night when all cats were gray.

Myself, I never charged commission like the saleswomen in the big stores who are paid a percentage of what they sell, or like that priest in the Aveyron. *Guelte* is the word, a commission or percentage, and I looked it up one day. According to the dictionary, it derives from the German *Geld*. You might indeed think so. The editor of that dictionary hadn't hidden a Jew in his cellar during the war. *Guelte,* obviously, is from the Yiddish. The founders of the big department stores were called Bloch, like the draper, or Kahn, or Meyer, or Bader. The word was said to be German to sound more sophisticated.

Herman and I had signed no contract. Who would have profited by it? Herman saved his skin for two years, three months and twenty days — he very nearly saved it entirely — and I knew love. If Herman had rejected me, would I have evicted him from the cellar? Would I have said: Go on, get out! Go away if you can't do anything for me anymore! It would have been ignoble of me, and dangerous, too: the fact that I had hidden a Jew would be revealed, I'd have risked the Hôtel des Barres and all that followed.

I know Yiddish now, and I can say that *guelte* comes from גֵעלט, but I don't know many people with whom I can speak it. Yet the spoken language is simpler, because there's no problem with the written characters. I'm not going to move to New York just to avoid losing my Yiddish. I once met a Polish woman. Her parents had been caretakers in the Jewish quarter of Lublin before the war. All through her childhood she had played with Jewish children in the courtyard of the building where they lived, and she spoke fluent Yiddish. Usually she kept quiet about it, but she was happy to speak Yiddish to me, perhaps because I wasn't Jewish. She, too, thought I had a funny accent. It's not my fault that I taught German all my life. And that I liked teaching it.

Herman was unpredictable, always slightly distracted except when he was making love to me. When he read German poetry aloud (although quietly for fear of discovery) he seemed to me far away, in the East, surrounded by camels and palm trees, and we were a little like the fir and the palm tree in the poem *Ein Fichtenbaum steht einsam,* I the fir tree, he the palm. In German the fir is a masculine noun, the palm tree is feminine. He told me that this poem had been inspired by a passage in the Talmud, a traditional Jewish legend. The idea shocked me. Heine, the great German poet, was Jewish; yes, I knew that, but I hadn't thought much about it before I knew Herman. I would have to get used to the idea. The Talmud.

"It's a collection of laws and legends."

"People often call it a dangerous book."

"It addresses the question of whether, when Groynem's hen's egg is found in Yankl's barn, the egg belongs to Groynem or Yankl. Would you call that dangerous? It tells us that Moses stammered because when he was a child he picked up a hot coal and put it to his mouth. It's a civil code and a collection of fairy tales. That's the dangerous weapon you're talking about."

I didn't believe what Herman said about the Talmud. Surely a book couldn't get burned in public just for telling stories about chickens and eggs.

7

AFTER THE BOMBING of the barracks, the hunt for Resistance fighters in the region was stepped up. The Nazis put up posters bearing the names and photographs of wanted terrorists. They all had sinister expressions and impossible names. Zylbersztajn, Szulc, Sztokfisz. Messrs Sz; they were Jews. And in the middle of them one day there was a Friedberg, like Hans-Joachim, but with a different first name, Jean. Was Hans-Joachim Jewish? The idea had never crossed my mind. He was so German, so handsome. If he was Jewish, he couldn't have been sent to the Russian front, there was no risk of his screwing my sister Anne once she was shipped off there as a prostitute after Volker's death — one can always dream.

I had buried that adolescent memory. I had told myself a reassuring story: Hans-Joachim in the Hitler Youth, Hans-Joachim fighting for *Lebensraum*, Hans-Joachim on the Russian front. In fact, he would have left Germany in 1933, or 1936, or 1938 at the latest. Or he would have stayed in Heidelberg, and who knows what would have become of him? If he got out of the country, where did he go? To the United States? He spoke no English. To France, then? I looked more closely at the face on the poster; the photograph was blurred, I couldn't identify it. Was he this un-shaven Jean Friedberg? The Germans could hardly print a German first name on a Wanted poster, it would have been like confessing to their own madness. I stared at the face in the photograph. It could be his, but the photo was so dark, how could I know?

Was Hans-Joachim hiding somewhere in the region? The Roche-Noire plateau beyond the last farms was densely forested. There were some huts among the trees where the woodcutters lived when they came to cut down timber. We used to stop there in my childhood to eat a picnic on our Sunday walks. The huts are gone now, they've fallen into ruin, the roofs and walls have collapsed and the wood they were made of has rotted and returned to the earth. If you look hard you may find an iron nail or a forgotten tin flask. But during the war these huts still stood.

I decided that one day I would go up to the Roche-Noire plateau to find out. I'd have made discreet inquiries first; I knew that an old schoolfriend of my sister's who had turned out better than Anne was up there. And I might have met Hans-Joachim again, but what would I have done then? Taken him down into the cellar, too? There wasn't room for two. And they would have murdered one another, my two loves, like two great stags fighting to rule the herd. Hans-Joachim wouldn't have wanted to skulk underground. He had joined the Resistance, I thought. He was fighting proudly. He was German. If I had asked him, he'd have killed his fellow countryman on the second floor.

Hans-Joachim, my friend, my only friend, save me from that SS man, put a pickax through his back when he's sprawling on top of my sister, not too violently so as not to put it through Anne at the same time — or kill him in a duel, Prussian-style, whatever you like. I'd only have had to ask and he would have done it. While Herman — he never thought of emerging from his den, let alone tackling Volker. I didn't suggest that he might run for it. I might have been able to find him an escape route through my colleague Viallet who taught Latin and Greek. I had my suspicions of what he was doing at the time, and it was confirmed later, when he was made Companion of the Liberation, very stylish. Yes, I might have been able to find Herman a way out through Viallet, so that he could go and blow up bridges. But I wanted to keep him for myself. Yet he was not entirely heroic down in his cellar. I have spoken of my love, the fascination he exercised on me. I have said nothing about admiration.

XOXOX

The day when the insurance agent told me the story of my father and the German farmer's wife, I ought to have gone on with what I was saying, if only to see his face. "Everyone has to paddle his own canoe as he thinks fit. Personally I hid a Jew for the whole of the war so that I could screw him whenever I pleased. I fed him bit by bit, a piece of bread to go down on me. Meat was more expensive." He was an oddity, that insurance agent. It was blackening my father's memory to tell me that story. I ought not to have bought the car from him. He was the kind of dubious character of whom my father himself would have said, "I wouldn't buy a used car from that man." I did buy it, and it gave me no more trouble than any other car I've had, after all.

Learning about the Yiddish language this way, I also perfected my training in linguistics, as it would be called these days. Like the priest in the Aveyron region with his rabbi, though in his case it was theology. After the war I could have been an interpreter at the tribunals for all the Jewish survivors who arrived in droves from Poland and Russia, fleeing who knew what to go who knew where, a flea-ridden lot without a word of French. So where did you learn Yiddish? Down in a cellar during the war. I kept a private tutor imprisoned there. Let me explain. Well, as it happens, I'm explaining to you now. But after the war I didn't want to take

my linguistic knowledge any further. I wanted to forget
Hans-Joachim, Herman, Volker, Anne's loud cries up on the
second floor, her sobs when she was raped in the middle of
the road, the doors and windows of our house sealed for several months.

When the Liberation came it wasn't easy to explain about
the SS man on the second floor and the Jew in the cellar.
And later the SS man in the cellar, too. Because I never did
get in touch with my sister's childhood friend, or go looking
for Hans-Joachim on the Roche-Noire plateau. I went on
dreaming that he was hiding in the region, I imagined him
very close to me. When I cycled along the streets in town,
on a bike which carried no coded messages for the Resistance, Hans-Joachim would be looking down at me from an
attic window, or up through a sewer grate.

It was simple, he was living in broad daylight under a
false identity, Henri-Jacques Fédeau — he'd kept the same
initials so that his monogrammed handkerchiefs wouldn't
give him away. He watched me pass, but I didn't see him. He
was there, only a few yards away, but he couldn't make himself known to me because of the war. He remembered me,
the university, Heidelberg, Thomas Mann and the castle of
the baroness with her emu feathers. He wanted to call out
my first name, I'd have turned around, I'd have recognized
his voice merely by that cry from the heart, I'd have run
back to him, and we'd have met again in the middle of the
street, in my native town where everyone knew me, more
than ten years after saying goodbye in Heidelberg. But

Hans-Joachim couldn't call my name. Even in broad daylight and under a false identity he was muzzled, like Herman down in the cellar.

Hans-Joachim never came. Whether he was in the region or not, I never saw him again, dead or alive. When I stopped imagining that he might come down from the Roche-Noire plateau to liberate me from Volker, I stopped expecting anyone else to do it. I killed the SS man with a blow from a kitchen cleaver, just as I'd said. I don't know what came over me, but someone had to finish the man off, didn't they?

Anne had gone out on urgent business, welcoming Cocteau to the municipal theater. Volker had turned up as usual. My mother was out on my bike, which she had borrowed; a cousin in the country had promised her a rabbit, and she was planning to make it for next Sunday's lunch. I was in the kitchen. I had put on water for a lime-blossom herb tea (an herb tea once in a while doesn't amount to a habit), and as I waited for it to boil, I was admiring the big cherry tree in the garden, which gave us wonderful fruit even in the war. My mother made cherry clafoutis without much batter; today we'd call it a gratin of red summer fruit and it would sound trendy, but at the time we didn't really enjoy the flavor of the cooked cherries, we thought only of the flour and eggs we so sorely missed.

I saw the SS cap coming up the steps of the porch by the window, and suddenly it was all too much for me, I'd had enough, I had to get rid of the man, whatever it cost the family. This decision, or rather impulse, came to me with the obvious realization that a chance like this wouldn't come my way again, me face-to-face with Volker (though not too close, all the same). I had no time to break a flowerpot over his head; with his cap on, it might not have killed him, and there were the neighbors to think of, too. I wanted to have him facing me, strike him as he deserved, even if he was much taller than me.

My blood was up, I opened the drawer of the kitchen table, I was trembling, but it all happened very fast. I had no time to tell myself this is madness, it can't be done, I'm risking my life. I took out the cleaver my mother used to cut up chickens and ducks (which as everyone knows go on running about after their heads are cut off, apparently it's a reflex), and at the moment when Volker appeared in the doorway I struck him a blow in the middle of his forehead: take that, chicken. Volker collapsed without a sound; it's so simple to kill a man. Not much blood came out, which made it easier to clean up afterwards. What did those SS men eat to give them such thick blood?

I had killed with a sure hand. Volker had fallen at my feet; I was trembling like a leaf. Fear suddenly came over me, breaking in on me, possessing me from head to foot. I was terrified. What joy did I have from killing Volker? None. Volker was even more in the way dead than alive. On his two feet (and even on all fours, sprawled above my sister) he had protected the house from prying eyes. Dead, he put us all in danger. I couldn't get him out of the house because of the neighbors. I undressed him; an SS uniform might come in handy. What surprised and almost disappointed me — one sometimes gets such odd ideas — was that his penis was of normal size.

I wrapped him in a sheet so as not to leave too much mess around the place, I dragged him to the cellar stairs, where I had to hold him so that he didn't topple down too fast, I unblocked the entrance to the hiding place, I went down first myself and then pulled Volker in by his feet. Herman wasn't expecting me; it was still daylight outside. I said: Here, now all we have to do is bury him, I'll go and get a shovel. Herman did not understand what the naked body was doing there. He looked at the death's head tattooed on the corpse's shoulder without reacting.

"Let me introduce Volker, almost one of the family, my sister's lover. I don't know if he's read Heine, I avoided talking to him, and it's too late to ask. His snores won't bother you now."

"What are you going to do with him?"

"I told you, we're going to bury him. Or rather you are. I must go back up and clean up the house. He bled a bit."

Since Herman was proving totally passive, I took the initiative for once. I brought down the spade and the SS uniform; I'd have to wash the bloodstains off it later with soap and water; I could hardly take it to the dry cleaners. I washed the floors upstairs, the kitchen, the corridor, and the stairs down to the cellar. I hadn't finished cleaning up when my mother came back. She said: What on earth are you doing? I was going to lie, say it was some whim or fancy, I suddenly felt the urge to do housework, but she saw Volker's cap on the hall dresser beside her grandmother's big porcelain platter, the cap of a man who had been both a member of the SS and her daughter's lover: it was reflected in the mirror. I had forgotten it. The cap was intact; Volker had taken it off a moment before I struck him with the cleaver.

"Did you kill him?"

"Yes."

"Where is he?"

"Never mind."

"What about Anne?"

"SS men are born, they live, they die."

My mother wouldn't talk. She was the essence of neutrality. Volker had vanished into thin air, and his disappearance remained an unexplained mystery. The Germans had other things to think about. The Allies were only a few hundred miles away, so they had to concentrate on the priorities: packing up, making sure of their retreat route, deporting the last Jews. Some soldiers were deserting, maybe that was what Volker had done. My sister wouldn't calm down. Volker had left without saying good-bye. What an insult from the Boche! After a few days I saw her fidgeting in an obscene sort of way, and in less than a week she had found herself another one, like her late husband a former member of the League of French Volunteers, a man who had miraculously survived the Eastern front. He limped from a war wound, but his other capacities were intact, at least to judge by my sister's whoops up on the second floor.

Herman did as I said. He buried Volker's body at my command. At first he was reluctant, he didn't want to share his quarters with the SS man, but the cellar was the only place in this house where you could dispose of a body. Up in the attic Volker would soon have been stinking the whole place up, and the garden was unthinkable, for even if the earth below the cherry tree soon consumed the German's flesh, the roots of the tree would encyst his skeleton. Herman had tried to persuade me to bury him in the wine cellar on the other side of the partition, but that would have been dangerous, and when he realized that I was not to be moved, he did the job. Time was in my favor, because Volker would soon start decomposing.

The ground under the cellar was soft; our house was situated at a bend in the river and built on alluvial soil; a glance at the garden confirmed this geological diagnosis, for its vegetation was luxuriant. If you spat a cherry stone out in the grass, four years later you could pick enough fruit to make dozens of jars of jam. Before the war my father spent his time pruning the trees in the late winter, and we burned the wood on the hearth indoors. We were almost self-sufficient in fuel, which was why our house was a little warmer than other people's during the war, except that some of our firewood was requisitioned. It was a good house, a family property built in 1905 by my maternal grandparents in country that was covered with market gardens at the time.

As the years went by, country lost out to town. Other houses were built, the fields of leeks and lettuce became a respectable middle-class district where teachers, municipal employees, and some shopkeepers lived. The Jews lived closer to the center, between the avenue Victor-Hugo and the place Giraudy, named for a mayor during the Second Empire and called by some the place Yihoudi. Since the beginning of the Occupation it had become the place of the Closed Shutters. The doors of the apartments had been sealed and their owners were gone. Gone to Switzerland, hiding in cellars like moles, or sent to the Hôtel des Barres and never heard of again. And there I was with my Jew in our cellar. I never thought of Jews before the war, or almost never — well, when I passed the place Giraudy I used to look through the tall windows at the big crystal chandeliers inside the apartments, and I couldn't help thinking that those houses were inhabited by Jews, but that was all. With Herman in the cellar, the subject became and has remained an obsession of mine. I have that Jew in me now — that Herman — and forever. He even passed his language on to me in the bargain.

XOXOX

When we had filled up Volker's hole (I helped Herman with that part of it), I said: We could grow salad stuff here, like in the old days. Herman added: Endive. And mushrooms, nice white mushrooms; in the absence of any Croix de Guerre we could always win a medal for the whitest mushrooms at the next agricultural fair. We had easily turned our plot of arable land, the same soil on which we used to lie so often making love. We'd made that beaten ground our little ploughed field.

Volker wasn't worth a Mass, he had died like a cow in the abattoir, one blow of the cleaver and it was all over, not even a moo. I remember the sound of his body collapsing softly on the walnut floorboards of the hall. Flop. Volker had vanished into thin air, no one knew where he had gone, and I've kept quiet about it until today. Back in Germany, there was a mother who didn't know what had become of her son, a wife who hoped for years that her husband would come back. She would jump whenever there was a knock on the door and stop herself from saying *das ist Volker,* but she ran to open it, hoping, and it would be the mailman, the woman who came around selling cheese, the rep from the Henckel laundry products company with his animal fat soaps, the man come to read the gas meter, never Volker.

His children were very small when he joined the SS. A boy and a girl, or two boys, it doesn't matter, blond, very blond, so blond as to be almost transparent, and what's more their mother had been congratulated by the Führer in person on her children's blondness. She had framed the letter stamped with the imperial eagle, the eagle and the swastika, and had hung it over the fireplace where no one ever cooked meat because of the smell. She took the framed letter down when the Russians arrived and hid it in the attic, one of the few souvenirs of her short life with Volker.

The children, Helmut and Ursula, told people their father had gone to war, was on a crusade, they hadn't been told he was in the SS, and unlike some of their little friends whose fathers did come home, they wouldn't find the Schutzstaffel uniform by accident in a wardrobe in the attic when they were searching their grandmother's clothes to play dressup, and they wouldn't know that their father had been part of the German elite, the master race, good family men, model husbands who executed thousands of Jews with a bullet in the back of the neck as their victims stood on the edge of a pit, heroes who set fire to churches after shutting the whole population of a village inside them, thus ensuring a radiant future for their descendants in a world washed clean, and then relaxed over a nice cool beer when they got home after a long day's work. Volker's children would develop the average kind of guilt of young Germans after the war, for being part of a people that had tried by every available means to get rid of another, and who knew why? Perhaps just because that other people spoke a language close to theirs but less high-class, comprehensible but so un-Prussian that they had to dispose of this philological bastard, this other that was too alien. Helmut and Ursula would not develop the huge, monstrous guilt of the children of SS men, the offspring of fathers who sent birthday cards to their dear children inscribed *Ich liebe dich, dein Vati* on coming home from work, and work meant liquidating twenty gypsies, fifty Jews and ten homosexuals, unless it was twenty cattle cars of gypsies, fifty cattle cars of Jews and ten cattle cars of homosexuals, they remember only numbers now, not the units of measurement, but what did it matter so long as the sum came out right? How many people did Volker kill during the war, how many boys did he torture, how many girls did he rape? How many sisters did he fuck?

Volker's children knew nothing about all that because their father's uniform stayed in France, not in the cellar with their father's body but somewhere else. Where?

Ought I to have exhumed Volker's skeleton after the war and sent it back to Frau Hammerschimmel, bones carefully arranged in a big box, skull on top of them, a discreet and tactful reminder of the tattoo on Volker's shoulder and the elegant crest on his cap?

8

HERMAN DIDN'T LIKE HAVING the SS man buried under him. He couldn't sleep, and within a few days he became very nervous after having patiently borne his isolation so long. Now the cellar floor burned under his feet. I was beginning to regret making him accept Volker's presence, making him live in a graveyard. We no longer made love, Herman didn't feel like it, he didn't seem to want me anymore. I tried to stimulate him, without success. His cock lay limp in my hands, between my lips, and he waited with a touch of annoyance for me to get discouraged.

"I can't live with that corpse."

"Forget him, he's not there, he never lived."

"I feel him here all the time. He's sending me mad. It

stinks of death in here. Look, the floor's not smooth the way it used to be, there's a bump, anyone can see where he's buried. The demons will soon come up."

"What are you talking about?"

"Haven't you ever noticed the lights in cemeteries by night? When I was little I sometimes went to visit my grandmother in the country. She lived close to the graveyard, and I went roaming around there at night."

"Those are will o' the wisps."

"They're demons, I tell you."

Strange beliefs for a man who loved Heine.

Herman was suffocating. The Allies were a hundred or so miles away, the Boche were in retreat. Herman threatened to come up from the cellar in broad daylight, just like that; he would climb the stairs one morning and ask my sister to make him a cup of coffee. I said: You're mad. He replied: Well, wouldn't you call burying an SS man in that cellar mad?

It was becoming impossible to prevent him from going out. I thought I might be able to find him another hiding place, where he could wait for the town to be liberated, but he would have to leave the house, the neighbors were on the lookout, and all would be revealed. It had been pure luck that no one had seen us coming in when I rescued Herman and settled him into the cellar. Old Madame Christophe

used to sit on her balcony from morning to evening in this
fine late summer weather.

Herman couldn't go out in the day, and it was risky at
night, for the curfew was still in force. I would have liked
him to stay in the cellar, but if he was withdrawing from me
it was no good keeping him isolated there. I agreed to get
him out. I thought of the SS uniform. There was a lot of
coming and going in this house, because of Anne. Herman
could escape at twilight, as darkness fell, that was when old
Madame Christophe went in to eat her dinner, and the
other neighbors wouldn't know the difference because of the
uniform. I put the idea to him. Herman hated the cellar so
much that he agreed.

"Shall we ever see each other outside this cellar? Will you
ever make love to me again?"

"France will soon be free."

That was just what I feared. Herman would owe me
nothing anymore, and would he still love me? Did it matter
if he loved me? The Liberation would bring no good with it,
and it was bound to part us.

I helped him put Volker's uniform on. It was well cut. I
can't say it suited him, but the seams were solid and well
sewn. The Nazis took a lot of trouble dressing their SS men.
The manufacturer had a good stylist, the fashion house of
Boss, from what I had heard. Hugo Boss can compete in el-
egance with the greatest French couturiers today thanks to
his father, who got the job from Hitler of clothing the SS

from Dunkirk to Crete. He was able to practice his technique, perfect his patterns, and try out his sewing machines on tens of thousands of uniforms. In remembrance of the Führer from a grateful haute couture industry.

Herman as Volker, I couldn't bear it, particularly the cap. Seeing my horror, Herman laid it on. He stood at attention, clicked his heels and goose-stepped up and down the cellar. Volker was lying just below him.

I stuffed Herman's clothes and shoes in a bag and hid them under a tree on the banks of the river, not far from a bridge, at a place where few people ever went. I told Herman how to get there. It was easy. Around eight darkness began to fall, and Herman left the cellar. It was a little later than expected; my sister had hung about in the sitting room before going upstairs. My mother was still in the kitchen, but I knew she would go on keeping quiet. Herman climbed the stairs, crossed the hall and passed the kitchen. He respectfully saluted my mother, who was alarmed to see an SS man come up from the cellar, an SS man who was not Volker, Volker resuscitated but not entirely him, not her own SS man, the one she had had to get used to, but another, taller, better-looking man. This was not the time for explanations. Herman went out. From the sitting-room window I saw him quietly open the garden gate. He closed it calmly, turned and went on his way. All I could see was the brown collar at his neck, a real SS man, or he could be taken for one. He turned right, as I had told him to, and disappeared round the corner of the road.

My mother was polishing. She went to close the cellar door and put the key in her pocket. She asked no questions that day, nor on the days that followed. When she died twenty-four years later, we had still never mentioned the SS man who walked down the corridor. That was my mother all over, a machine for swallowing reality and never spitting it out again; she was like a large container, and spent her life filling herself up with everything she thought it best to hide, to bury, those ardent truths that are strewn through one's life and are fatal if they are left unused. My mother died of cancer of the colon. She would have liked to be buried in the garden of the house her parents had built at the bend of the river, but the law wouldn't allow it in peacetime, or what was called peacetime, peace on the outside anyway, when there were graveyards for the dead.

Our cellars have never been restored to their centuries-old function because people no longer store potatoes, they buy them every day in the supermarket instead. Cellars and laundry rooms are no use anymore. They fill up with worn-out items that people think they may bring out someday, but when they do, the old junk has gone moldy, smells strongly of saltpeter and is fit only to be thrown out. Our house's laundry room is not used anymore. It still has the big stone sink where my grandmother washed linen, but no water has flowed into it for several decades. A pipe has been fixed to the tap to water the garden. The sink itself has been covered with a washboard on which a tiny cauldron stands, not the big one where my grandmother boiled the linen — goodness knows what became of that one after the invention of washing machines — but a toy given to my mother when she was a little girl. That little cauldron is all that's left of the furnishings of a whole doll's house.

I hide the spare keys in there, half the town knows that's where they are, you only have to lift the lid and the metal mushroom valve which made the water go round, and there are the keys underneath. The little cauldron was already in the laundry room during the Occupation, but on a shelf above the sink where the washing was still done, and the keys were inside. We feared many things during the war, but not strangers breaking into the house by night. I was slightly afraid that a burglar might get in, go down to the cellar and find Herman, but I couldn't ask my mother to take the keys out of the little cauldron. I'd always seen them there, and my request would have seemed suspect.

After Herman had left the house in his SS uniform, I followed him in my mind, going the way I had told him. Down rue Matignon, then left onto rue Mordillat, straight ahead to the place du Sacré-Coeur, then onto the rue des Bons-Enfants, take the path level with No. 18, the towpath, the tree, the bag. Herman undresses in the dark, gets rid of that assassin's uniform which has saved his life and finds his human garments. Herman in his underclothes on the banks of the river. Is he wearing mine or Jude's this evening? It's summer. The crescent moon is reflected, distorted, in the dark water. It casts its tender moonbeams on Herman's body, which I have never seen in that soft light, I know it only down in a cellar smelling of enclosed space, dust, trodden earth. The riverbank smells of grass wet with dew, fresh mint, walnut leaves. And the river flows on. The heat of summer does not dry up the watercourses in this mountainous country, it melts the glaciers, and the river carries away the muddy water from the peaks, together with branches, tree trunks and sometimes, at this time of war when it's easy to settle personal accounts, sometimes corpses.

Herman never reached the end of the route I had planned for him. My telepathic guidance didn't work as I had hoped. The system seized up halfway. He fell in the rue des Bons-Enfants outside No. 12, brought down by submachine-gun fire. A member of the Resistance trying to bag an SS man a few days before the Liberation. One man fired, another fell. Jean Friedberg, maybe, at one end of the weapon, Herman at the other, shot down I don't know why. I have spent forty years trying to get him the honor officially due to a man who "died for France," but unsuccessfully. I don't know why I spent so many years fighting the civil service for it, since that honor would have done no one any good. Herman died childless, at least as far as I know.

In what category of the Ministry of Veterans would you

put a Jew killed wearing an SS uniform? War isn't a fancy-dress party. Everyone in war has his job and must do it. The Resistance fighter resists, the Jew hides, the sister spreads her legs and waits for her German lover, and I — well, I floated about among these characters, a branch eaten away by rot, a piece of wood abandoned to the river. I had never known love before; I found love in the middle of the war. I lost my love in the last hours of the Occupation. It's absurd. And suppose Herman had survived? Would I have set up house with him? That's even more absurd.

Herman ended up in the river. At the time, I couldn't stomach the idea of going to recover his body and give him a decent burial. You have to imagine yourself in the same context: who would have dared to pick up the corpse of an SS man and risk suffering the same fate? Only an Antigone. It wasn't until after the Liberation that I told the whole story, and even then it wasn't easy, for our country accepts only one true story, the story of the heroes, the conquerors, those who from the first had been fighting in a Resistance that never before had as many members as it did in 1945.

After the war I waited for Madame Bloch the draper to return, but she never did, or not as far as I know. My remorse for letting her walk past me remained with me for a long time, and I dared not revive her memory. So I did not think about it, but all the same it lurked inside me, crouching in a corner ready to leap out. I thought only of Herman, and I thought a little of Hans-Joachim, too. I suffered from heartburn over a long period; it must have been Madame Bloch.

I went on teaching German — what else could I do? My mother is dead, my father is dead, my sister Anne died in her car on a main road, trying to pass a truck, but another truck was coming toward her and they met head-on. She crashed into the truck radiator. The truck driver was terrified, and my sister's death as she drove full speed along that country road may have traumatized him for life. I live here in my mother's house. I don't look after it as well as she did, it's too big for me, all I use is my bedroom, my study and the bathroom on the second floor, and the kitchen a little. The sitting room on the first floor is full of dust, like the other rooms. They drowse away, waking up once a year when my sister Isabelle — still very energetic for her age, and she's six years older than me — comes for All Saints' Day with her children and grandchildren. Now that her parents and sister are in the graveyard, Isabelle always makes that pilgrimage. She is head of a fine and very lively family, it's a pleasure to see them.

I have been retired for over twenty years. After May 1968 the high school became coeducational. I've taught German to half the town. My first pupils have now themselves retired. I sometimes see some of my old students on television, others send me good wishes once a year. They even included a government minister not so long ago. His father was in the Milice paramilitaries during the Occupation. A nose for politics is passed from one generation to the next.

With the years the memory of Madame Bloch has surfaced in me again. I tried to trace her. What had happened to her after I saw her for the last time at the Hôtel des Barres? I was unable to get access to the archives, which were closed to the public for several decades. At the end of the 1970s I read an article in the newspaper about a work which had just been published, the *Memorial of the Deportation of the Jews of France,* a kind of directory listing the Jews who had been deported. I didn't find Madame Bloch's name there. I didn't know exactly where to look, because after being arrested in our town she would have been sent to Drancy or some other French internment camp. There are more than seventy-five thousand names in that book, and hundreds of Blochs. I've spent years going through the pages of the directory, hoping to find her.

> Blaywas Joseph
> Blazer David
> Bloch Jacques
> Bloch Joseph
> Bloch Toni
> Blochowa Max
> Block Marcel
> Blum Johanna

Blum Léopold
Blum Samuel
Blumenfeld Oscar

Those pages full of names sent me back to the list of strong
verbs I had learned at school:

backen	buck	gebacken
beginnen	began	begonnen
beissen	biss	gebissen
bergen	barg	geborgen
bieten	bot	geboten
binden	band	gebunden
bitten	bat	gebeten
blasen	blies	geblasen
bleiben	blieb	geblieben
braten	briet	gebraten
brechen	brach	gebrochen

As I went through the lists, my eye happened to fall on the
former owner of the dictionary of Yiddish literature now in
my library: Moszek Cymbalista, born in Mogielnica on
March 2, 1902, Polish by nationality. Deported on June 28,
1942, from Beaune-la-Rolande in the Loiret area. The
records show that the convoy consisted of 1,038 deportees.
At the Liberation, thirty-five of them survived. In the same
train, perhaps in the same truck, there was a Blok with a *k*,
first name Jeches, born in Warsaw on June 12, 1905.

Every August 10 I go down to the river and the place where Herman was to have changed his clothes after leaving the cellar. I sit on the damp ground, I watch the muddy water flow by for several hours, I linger there. It is my memorial ceremony for Herman, my little *Shma-Yisroel,* as he used to say. Soon I won't be able to do it anymore. You are as old as your arteries. So then I shall think of him without leaving my room. The tall branches of the acacia will help me to conjure up his memory.

The house is changing. Every time Isabelle's children come they bring a little more clutter into the place. My mother's image is fading from the walls of her home. Am I being nostalgic? The cellar is just as it was. The furniture, the books, the beaten earth floor. The air down there is very dry, and everything is perfectly preserved. I imagine that my nephews went down there on purpose when they were little, to give themselves a fright. Great fun for children. They haven't said anything about it to me, have asked me no questions. Later, after my death, they will try to reconstruct the past. Perhaps not all of them; some won't want to know. Will they go so far as to dig up the cellar floor? One of them, or one of their children, will probably end up in the lunatic asylum; someone has to take the rap for the others in a family.

There is one place left in the cemetery, in the family vault, which takes six. It already holds my maternal grandparents, my parents, and an aunt who died young. My sister

Anne was buried beside her husband in his family's vault. Isabelle will be buried with her in-laws in the southwest of the country. Jude is with mine on the other side of the graveyard. I am the only one yet to join the others. But what have I to do with any of these people? My place is with Herman, nowhere. I have scribbled a will on a piece of paper. My earthly goods to Isabelle and her children, a little extra for Alfred because he is my godson. And my body to the fire. I have asked to be cremated. It will be my last thought of Madame Bloch.

Appendix

Translated material

From page 18:

Death in Venice, a novella by Thomas Mann. Chapter 1.
On a spring afternoon in 19–, the year in which for months
on end so grave a threat seemed to hang over the peace of
Europe, Gustav Aschenbach, or von Aschenbach as he had
been officially known since his fiftieth birthday, had set out
from his apartment on the Prinzregentenstrasse in Munich
to take a walk of some length by himself.

From page 38:

> Thou who from the heavens art
> Soothe our grief and pain, we pray,

Filling every wretched heart
With refreshment on its way.

From pages 69 and 70:

A fir stands tall and lonely
On barren northern heights.
It slumbers in white covers
Of freezing snow and ice.

The fir dreams of a palm tree
In distant eastern lands,
Silent, alone, in mourning
On burning rocks it stands.

From page 84:

Fairest cradle of my sorrow
Fairest tombstone of my peace,
City fair, we part tomorrow,
Adieu, I cry without surcease.

From page 109:

I have a blue piano in my home
I can't play a tune or song.
It stands in the dark by the cellar door
Now that the world's gone wrong.

Four starry hands play, tingle-tangle
— the moon in the boat sang along —
and now the rats join the jingle-jangle.

The piano keyboard broke in pain . . .
I mourn the blue dead.
Dear angels, open the door again
— I have eaten bitter bread —
open the door of heaven once more
even against the law.

From pages 114 and 115:
Well watered by all my tears
Many fair flowers will spring,
And I will sigh no more, instead
The nightingales will sing.

Dear child, if you will love me
The flowers shall tell our tale
And at your window you shall hear
The lovely nightingale.

Literary Citations

Heinrich Heine, "Ein Fichtenbaum steht einsam." Translated into Yiddish by Ruvn Ayzland in *Di verk fun Haynrikh Hayne, zekster band: dos bukh fun lider*, Yiddish, New York, 1918, p. 112.

Heinrich Heine, "Schöne Wiege meiner Leiden," in *Heines Werke, erster Teil: Buch der Leider*, Berlin, Deutsches Verlagshaus Bong & Co., p. 90. Translated into Yiddish by Naftole Gros in *Di verk fun Haynrikh Hayne, zekster band: dos bukh fun lider*, Yiddish, New York, 1918, p. 46.

Heinrich Heine, "Aus meinen Tränen spriessen" (2nd song in "Lyrisches Intermezzo"), in *Heines Werke, erster Teil: Buch der Leider*, Berlin, Deutsches Verlagshaus Bong & Co., p. 124.

Translated into Yiddish by Mani Leyb in *Di verk fun Haynrikh Hayne, zekster band: dos bukh fun lider,* Yiddish, New York, 1918, p. 99.

Else Lasker-Schüler, "Mein blaues Klavier," in *Sämtliche Gedichte.* Reprinted by permission of Suhrkamp Verlag.

Thomas Mann, *Death in Venice and Other Stories,* translated by David Luke, published by Martin Secker & Warburg/ Vintage. Reprinted by permission of The Random House Group, Ltd.

ABOUT THE AUTHOR

Gilles Rozier was born in Grenoble in 1963. He is
the director of the center for Yiddish culture in
Paris. This is his third novel.

ABOUT THE TRANSLATOR

Anthea Bell was educated at Somerville College, Oxford. Her translations from German and French include works of nonfiction, literary and popular fiction, and books for young people. Recent translations from German include E. T. A. Hoffmann's *The Life and Opinions of the Tomcat Murr* (Penguin Classics, 1999), W. G. Sebald's *Austerlitz* (Hamish Hamilton, 2001), and Sigmund Freud's *The Psychopathology of Everyday Life* (Penguin, 2002). Translations from French include a number of novels by Henri Troyat. She has received several translation awards, including the Schlegel-Tieck award three times, the Independent Foreign Fiction Prize and the Helen and Kurt Wolff Prize (U.S.A.) for the translation of W. G. Sebald's *Austerlitz,* and the 2003 Austrian State Prize for Literary Translation.

mains
22r98

WITHDRAWN